CONTE

Milet Publishing
333 North Michigan Avenue
Suite 530
Chicago IL 60601
info@milet.com
www.milet.com

First published by Milet Publishing Ltd in 2005
Copyright © Milet Publishing Ltd, 2005
Foreword copyright © Philip Pullman, 2005

Cover and inside illustrations by Pablo Bernasconi.

A catalogue record of this book is available from the British Library.

ISBN 1 84059 487 X

Milet's distributors are as follows:

UK & Ireland
Turnaround Publisher Services, Unit 3, Olympia Trading Estate,
Coburg Road, London N22 6TZ

North America & Latin America
Tuttle Publishing, 364 Innovation Drive, North Clarendon, VT 05759-9436

Australia & New Zealand
Tower Books, Unit 2/17 Rodborough Road, Frenchs Forest NSW 2086
Global Language Books, PO Box 108, Toongabbie NSW 2146

South Africa
Quartet Sales & Marketing, 12 Carmel Avenue,
Northcliff, Gauteng, Johannesburg 2195

The opinions, selections and reviews in this book are those of the editors,
contributors and reviewers and not those of Milet Publishing.

This book was published with the assistance of the Arts Council England.

Printed and bound in Malta by Compass Press

Acknowledgements

A special thank you to everyone who contributed to this publication:
Sarah Adams, Pablo Bernasconi, Patricia Billings, Bridget Carrington,
Klaus Flugge, Laura Hambleton, Neal Hoskins, Lene Kaaberbol,
Oliver Keen, Gillian Lathey, Inma Magan, Philip Pullman, Elizabeth Strick,
Nicholas Tucker, Sedat Turhan. And also to the many people who have
given support and advice: Chris Brown, Wendy Cooling, Nikki Gamble, Terence Ellis,
Ann Lazim, Nicky Potter, Michael Rosen, Siân Williams, Turnaround Publisher Services and
all the publishers who have submitted books for inclusion in this guide.

This publication could not have come about without the support of Arts Council England,
Milet Publishing and the Children's Bookshow.

Arts Council England supports a range of literature projects through our funding scheme,
Grants for the arts, and through our portfolio of regularly funded organisations. We recognise
the transforming power of the arts in relation to young people and place cultural diversity at
the heart of our work.

Milet Publishing publishes a leading list of bilingual books for children, featuring hundreds
of popular titles in English with over 25 languages, and a celebrated range of artistic,
innovative and award-winning children's books in English, many of which are translated from
other languages.

The Children's Bookshow was set up in 2003 by Siân Williams and is supported by Arts
Council England. It is a national tour of children's writers and illustrators who perform in
theatres throughout England during October and November of each year. A programme of
school workshops runs alongside the tour. Each tour has a theme and has included Poetry,
Folk and Fairy Tales and Translation.

Editors

Deborah Hallford is a freelance project consultant specialising in children's literature and arts
projects. She previously co-edited *Folk and Fairy Tales: A Book Guide* with Edgardo Zaghini,
published by Booktrust. Deborah worked at Booktrust for over 15 years where she was
Head of Publications from 2001–March 2005. She has an M.A. in History and is a Committee
member of IBBY UK (International Board on Books for Young People).

Edgardo Zaghini is a specialist in children's literature having previously co-edited *Folk and Fairy
Tales*. He was the commissioning editor for a wide range of children's literature publications and
information officer at Booktrust for eight years. Edgardo has an M.A. in Children's Literature, is
a chartered librarian and author of *Pop-Ups: A Guide to Novelty Books* and *The Children's
Book Handbook*. He has been a Committee member of IBBY and the CBHS (Children's Books
History Society).

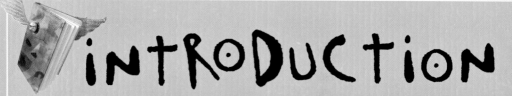 iNTRODUCTiON

Deborah Hallford & Edgardo Zaghini, Editors

'Our children need to be exposed to a world of voices so that the whole world becomes their home'
David Almond, speech at the 2003 *Marsh Award for Children's Literature in Translation*, School Librarian, Spring 2003

The intention of this publication is to celebrate and actively promote an interest in the rich tradition and culture of children's literature from around the world. We hope that it will be a useful resource containing information about which books are currently available in translation, biographical details of authors, illustrators and translators and a resource guide.

Included in the book are a foreword by Philip Pullman and articles written on topics that will help to stimulate the debate surrounding the subject of translation: Nicholas Tucker explores why there is a British problem in the translation of children's books; Sarah Adams writes about 'Translating Monsters', her experience of translating the Golem books; Lene Kaaberbol identifies some of the problems of being translated and of being a translator; Gillian Lathey discusses teaching an MA module on children's literature in translation at Roehampton University; Patricia Billings explores bilingual books, and Klaus Flugge and Neal Hoskins give two different publishing perspectives.

Our literary heritage is made up of many books that are only known to us in translation from the Bible and Aesop's Fables to classics from authors such as Tolstoy, Kafka, Camus, Calvino and many more. Edgardo Zaghini's article on classic European children's books highlights the vast wealth of literature that has been opened up to new readers through translation.

Translated literature should break down the barriers of geography, language, race and build bridges between nations. It can develop a greater tolerance and understanding of other people's beliefs by teaching us about other cultures, and it can be an enriching experience as it opens up new horizons and stimulates ideas.

Out of the 3% of all books published in the UK each year that are translated, only 1% are children's books. Contrasted sharply with other countries in Europe such as France, where a quarter of all books published are translations and 35% in the Netherlands and Germany, this reveals a wide difference between the UK and the rest of Europe. This highlights the need for raising the profile of children's literature in translation in the UK, particularly if we don't want children to remain isolated and narrow minded about other cultures.

We have tried to bring together, in one unique volume, a selection of children's books in translation (all in print at the time of going to press). It has been impossible to include everything, but we hope we have provided a broad cross-section of titles that will appeal to everyone.

How to use the guide

Outside In has been divided into eight sections: five age categories, graphic novels, non-fiction and dual-language sections. The age categories are under 5; 6–8; 9–11; 12+ and 14+. Within each category the books are listed in order of age rather than alphabetically (with the exception of 14+ which is alphabetical by title). This is intended to act only as a broad guideline; in fact, many of the books will appeal to a wider age-range, including adults.

In partnership with Milet Publishing and the Children's Bookshow and supported by Arts Council England, we have been able to produce a guide that we hope will make a difference.

FOREWORD Phillip Pullman

© James Pullman

The subject of books available in English translation usually resolves itself into a question: why are there so few of them?

Because there are: disgracefully few. Shamefully few. And fewer than there used to be, too, at a time when publishers are putting out more books than ever. Only about 3% of the books on the UK market are translations, compared with about 23% in France. It's as if something has happened to our understanding of the world, making it narrower and less interested in the experience of elsewhere.

Part of the reason for this is the astonishing success of the English language, which grew out of Latin and Anglo-Saxon and French and absorbed words from hundreds of other sources: Hindi, Turkish, Swedish, Hungarian, Indonesian . . . There are traces, in our rich and cross-bred language, of the contact we've had with almost every country in the world. And being a tough and healthy thing, as mongrels often are, the English language has wandered all over the place and now finds itself in daily use in the mouths of millions of people who have never been to England in their lives, and have no intention of coming here.

That means that there are plenty of books from other countries that were written in English to start with – books from the USA, from Canada, from Australia, from India, from New Zealand, from the Caribbean, from Africa – and which don't need translating; so from one point of view it looks as if there's nothing to worry about. What's more, other media use English relentlessly: the power of Hollywood and almost all TV and pop music and video games and the internet are transmitted to us through English, and those things are so strong and well-funded, and so intoxicatingly addictive, that they add to the impression that we needn't bother with anything else, with the different, the foreign, the strange: what can books in foreign languages possibly say to us? What do they matter? Why should we bother?

Some commentators say that it's paradoxical to find so little interest in literature from abroad in this age of globalization, but perhaps that's the very problem: globalization is a phenomenon that's driven by money and business, not by culture and curiosity. In more innocent times, publishing companies were set up by people who loved books, and published them because they thought they could make a decent living by offering them to the public. (It's interesting to see how many books in this list come from small independent publishers. Good for them!) But these days, more and more mainstream publishers are owned by big multi-national corporations that are interested only in profit, and in nothing else whatsoever.

And it costs money to translate books, because it's a demanding intellectual activity and there aren't many people who can do it well, and publishers are reluctant to spend money on producing books that booksellers won't sell, and booksellers are reluctant to give space to books that readers don't want, and readers don't want books they've never seen reviewed, and literary editors won't review books if the publishers don't spend much money on advertising, and publishers won't spend money on advertising because . . . And it all goes round in a circle, and outside the circle is the rest of the world.

Which is a great pity.

But there are some hopeful signs, one of which is the *Marsh Award for Children's Literature in Translation*. Another is the sense among many people who care for books (and that certainly includes individual publishers, booksellers, readers, and literary editors) that they would all *like* to be able to see books from foreign languages in English translation, if only everyone else would let them.

And another is a guide such as this. I'm very encouraged that such a thing is being produced, and I'm sure it will be welcomed by everyone in the field. As I looked through the first draft of the list I was glad to see some old friends as well as many names I'd never heard of.

Because books do become friends. What I hope is that this guide will help some child today to meet a book that will remain with them for the rest of their life – a story and some characters who will make an impression that never leaves them. Among the many books I read as a child, there were three translations that had that effect. One was the Moomin series by Tove Jansson, from Finland, translated by Elizabeth Portch and Thomas Warburton, another was a French novel by Paul Berna called *A Hundred Million Francs*, translated by John Buchanan-Brown, and the third was Erich Kästner's *Emil and the Detectives* from Germany, translated by Margaret Goldsmith.

What I found with those books was that reading them was like being at home in a strange land. Strange, because there were some things I didn't know about: never having been a working-class child in a dingy French suburb, I didn't know how things were done there, but my new friends soon showed me and welcomed me into their gang as we went careering down the hill astride the horse on wheels that turned out to contain a fortune; and never having been young and lost and penniless in Berlin, I wouldn't have had a clue how to manage if I hadn't been in the excellent company of Emil and Gustav and the Professor and Little Tuesday and all the rest of them. And never having had an enormous nose like a hippo, and a tail like a piece of string, I might have found the company of the Moomins a little exotic – except that they, like the others, made me welcome at once. They made me feel at home.

Books do that. What I would have missed, if I'd never encountered these lifelong friends! What fun I would never have known, if the publishers and booksellers and librarians of my childhood hadn't seen the value of putting books from foreign languages in front of an English child! There was a fashion in the early 1970s, when I began to teach, for saying that we should not offer children literary experiences that differed from their everyday lives. They could not relate to them, we were told; they would not be able to identify with characters from a different background; children from inner-city housing estates could only properly appreciate stories about children from inner-city housing estates, and so on. Sensible teachers and parents took no notice of this reductive and pessimistic attitude to the imagination, but it did have an effect. I wonder whether the attitudes of that period might still be persisting? Children who were being taught then are now coming to positions of influence in publishing and broadcasting and in the news media. You never know.

And you never know what will set a child's imagination on fire. Who would have guessed that an 11-year-old child in Albania fifty or more years ago would have been so excited by Macbeth that he copied it out into his notebook? That child was Ismail Kadaré, who was awarded the first *Man Booker International Prize* in 2005 for his lifetime's work. There are children today in this country who will find a book, or books, in this guide satisfying a hunger they didn't know they had, and exciting a passion they had no idea they were capable of feeling. We don't know who they are, and we don't know which books will have that effect; but if we DON'T offer children the experience of literature from other languages, we're starving them. It's as simple as that.

The fee for this foreword has been donated to the charity Kids Company who offer emotional and practical support to children who do not have a competent carer. They have created a service that is accessed by 4,500 children in 22 schools across London and through a children's centre at street level. A team of social workers, teachers, psychologists, artists and musicians help re-parent children and return them to a safer experience of childhood.

Children's Books in Translation; Why is there a British problem?

Nicholas Tucker

Publishers have to make money, and those in Britain who have tried translating children's books from abroad have often lost more than they have gained. This is not an invariable rule: think of the profits that must have accrued from *Heidi, Pippi Longstocking* and *The Diary of Anne Frank*. But in general, a picture book from a foreign illustrator or, even more problematic, a teenage novel from some-where in Europe both still have less chance of commercial success over here. Why?

One reason must be that there has for many years been an abundance of good books coming on to the market, making it less likely that publishers will look abroad while so much is going on at home. With their authors and illustrators on hand for publicity jaunts and school visits, these British books already have a built-in advantage in a country long unused anyway to looking abroad for inspiration. It would be different if the British spoke only a minority language or felt that their own culture was cutting them off from more interesting developments elsewhere. But buoyed up by centuries of uninvaded independence, the British have long been prone to think that foreigners are more likely to learn something from them rather than the other way round.

The experience of two World Wars also meant that many other European countries were either demonised, patronised or just laughed at during propaganda campaigns at the time and this applied to contemporary children's literature and lasted long after each war came to an end.Such vestigial distrust of abroad is still perceptible in those weary jokes about krauts and wops of the type that used once to amuse young readers of the war-time *Beano* and *Dandy* comics. This attitude also owes something to a centuries old Protestant distrust of Europe's Roman Catholic mainland. Or as geography book published for children in 1818 put it,

Q. Would not God be angr-y that I-tal-ians wor-ship i-dols and a piece of bread?

A. God is ang-ry.

Yet children themselves, before they have had time to absorb some of these noxious attitudes, are open to all sorts of literature coming their way. For them, especially when they are small, the whole world can seem like a foreign country where people are apt to do or say unaccountable things. Small children like returning to various favourite books to find some sense of order in what the psychologist William James, brother to the more famous Henry, termed 'the great blooming, buzzing confusion' typical of an infant's first impressions of the world. Nationality is the least of their problems when it comes to understanding others at a time when even their own uncle can on occasions seem seriously unpredictable.

It is no surprise, therefore, to find that popular nursery rhymes and fairy tales convey little or no sense of nationality. Cinderella comes over first and foremost as someone infants like and understand; which country she lives in is an irrelevance. Hansel and Gretel obviously sound foreign, but their war against the witch is universal. Animal characters tend to be equally stateless, living in their own anthropomorphic world. The fact that all fairy tale or picture book characters, foreign or otherwise, are invariably portrayed speaking English also makes them easy to assimilate. When infants encounter foreigners who only speak their own language, their response is to continue talking to them in English, but more loudly. The idea that anyone cannot understand a language that infants themselves can speak is for some time simply too difficult for them to contemplate.

Eventually children realise that other countries exist where things are sometimes done differently, and all the more interesting for that. Babar the Elephant, with his stylish city clothes and dinky car, is extra fascinating because he lives in two environments both so different from a British child's experience: the deep jungle and inter-war metropolitan France. And it is at this point, when child readers are ready for more advanced picture books, that Britain could be more so much more adventurous in primary school book provision. One long-term way of encouraging a suspicious electorate to take a more benign view of their partners in the EU could be to make sure that its children come across more picture books set in the other countries now linked together. If this sort of provision was deemed to need extra financial aid from a body like Ariane, the EU translation committee, so be it. Spending a tiny part of the EU budget on translating picture books from every member country and then making sure they were distributed across the board would surely make more sense than yet one more food subsidy.

Inadequately sampling a foreign culture can at times be even more misleading than knowing nothing about it at all. Brought up myself on Lucy Fitch Perkins' famous *Twins* series, I believed for some years that the Chinese wore pigtails and still bound children's feet and that all Dutch children wore clogs. But a translation of Erich Kästner's *Emil and the Detectives* proved more fruitful, at a time when British bombers were droning overhead night after night on their way to yet another saturation bombing exercise. What, I used sometimes to wonder, might be happening to boys like Emil, let alone his mother, his grandmother and all his friends? Simply realising that people abroad were still recognisably human was important when British newspapers carried slogans like

'The only good German is a dead German.' Erich Kästner, banned in his own country, was an important figure for many children in war-time Britain, particularly when it came to forming attitudes to post-1945 Germany. Years later, Philip Pullman claimed the same novel as one of his inspirations for his great trilogy, His Dark Materials.

Modern picture books and stories from the rest of Europe often take a bleaker view of world politics than is usual over here. Examples include Georges Lemoine's *La petite marchande d'allumettes,* Pef's *Une si jolie poupée* and Roberto Innocenti's *Rose Blanche.* This last title, appearing in Britain in 1985 with a text by Ian McEwan based on a story by Christophe Gallaz, is about a small child discovering the secret existence of a concentration camp outside her small town in Germany. Ending in one more tragedy, this beautiful and moving book has been universally well received by British teachers and critics. The two other titles I refer to, by Georges Lemoine and the self-styled Pef, both unforgettably allude to the recent war in Bosnia. Children who have the chance to read such books can only come away feeling wiser if a little sadder.

Abroad is not just about politics; it is also about different ways of seeing, feeling and behaving. Continental illustrators like Michael Sowya and Quint Buchholz carry with them an exciting whiff of subversion for readers used only to how things are at home. Authors like Gudrun Pausewang, Hans Magnus Enzensberger, Daniel Pennac and Ted van Lieshout, who are translated, do the same thing in print. *Vive la difference!* indeed, but how typical it is that this resounding phrase still as yet has no British equivalent!

Translating Monsters

Sarah Adams

A golem is a monster that risks getting the better of you. And there were times, in the eighteen months it took me to coax my virtual monsters across the Channel, when I felt like I was up against it. My roller-coaster research ride, from the Algerian quarter of Marseille to the heart of youth culture in Brixton, was exhilarating enough. But I hadn't bargained for the way the challenge would keep on morphing.

Following GOLEM's success in France (and in particular its appeal to reluctant boy readers), my job was to translate this pot-boiler adventure series, set in the contemporary urban ghetto, and make it work for a streetwise British readership. Which meant rolling up my shirtsleeves and tackling that ongoing tension between a faithful (dull?) translation and a promiscuous (gripping?) one. Let me give you a film analogy: unlike screen buffs, as a reader you don't get to choose whether you're perusing the original version with subtitles or the dubbed one. I have to make that decision for you. I'd like to think the British GOLEM works best where aspects of adaptation, original version and transparency all hang together.

Dealing with the non-nametag of myths can be liberating and bewildering for the translator. You may feel freer to forge a fresh voice in your mother tongue, but in the absence of a strong sense of how that voice was born, or what parameters shaped it, your translation risks becoming a slippery veneer of para-phrases. Here the three co-authors, aka the Murail siblings, took an oral tradition and transformed it into a fast-paced current serial, updating the tradition of the *roman feuilleton*

with comic-strip humour. In this process of writing *à six mains*, they didn't just forget which specific bits 'belonged' to them, but expressly extended this spirit of team-work (the French word 'collaboration' has too much of a negative connotation) to their British translator. They were happy to entertain the idea that, in addition to ferrying linguistic meaning, translation can also be about cultural fine-tuning, or the re-stacking of humour necessary to make stories work afresh.

One of the most legendary re-workings of the Golem myth was set in 16th Century Prague where Rabbi Loeb created a monster designed to help out the oppressed ghetto-dwellers, but which ended up destroying them instead. Fast forward some four hundred years, factor a few edgy themes into the equation – like voracious multinationals, mass consumerism, cyberspace and virtual babes – and you get the Murails' up-to-the-minute version, set against the backdrop of graffiti tags, hip-hop and North African immigration. The action takes place on a run-down housing project (the Paris suburbs are mentioned, but it could be any high density living area in any multicultural city of a developed country). The happy twist in the tale is one of urban regeneration.

Talking of which, here's an example of the kind of topographical headache I faced. The outskirts of French cities like Marseille are often scarred by housing projects that sprawl horizontally for 200m. These concrete 'barres' are now reckoned such an architectural and social disaster, the French government has begun dividing them up as well as demolishing them. So how do I convey all that in the term 'tower block'? Ghetto humour proved easier to translate. Like the way the more 'mashed up' (as in problematic) an estate is, the more absurdly up-beat its name: Hummingbird Tower, Flamingo Block, Paradise Estate.

It was the backslang I really had to get my teeth into. The French love turning their words back to front and inside out. So in verlan (the back-to-front way of saying *l'envers* which, you guessed it, means 'back to front') *a femme* becomes a meuf, a mec (guy) becomes a keum, a *prof(esseur)* is a *feupro* and *les flics* (police) are *keufs*. Take that last example: an old skool English translation would be 'pigs', but given the US influence on UK slang, you might want to refer to them as Feds or Five O's (as in Hawaii). There's a free-style factor going down here too. You don't just splice the words down the middle and flip 'em back to front – there's got to be a feeling, often a musical one, for what's best to add or subtract to make the word flow or jam. Just to keep everybody on their toes, *verlan* is now being re-reversed or double-flipped so that beur which is backslang for 'arabe' has been re-mixed to form '*rebeu*'. Where all this starts getting complicated is in absorbing the Maghreb influences from the French (the hard K sounds in verlan often give the words an Arabic feel), while looking to shades of, say, Jamaican patois in the English. I wanted the authenticity of dialogue from a Bali Rai novel, for example, rather than have my characters speaking the typecast ghetto fabulous of Ali G hybrids.

This kind of banter and wordplay is also much more encoded, systematic even, in French. Which makes interacting with mainstream culture much easier – once you've grasped the principle, you don't just understand what's been done to words but you've got the power to forge slang yourself. Such coded language in British culture tends to represent specific-interest groups, as with the gay language *Polari*. Like the English language itself, our mainstream slang tends to be a rich melting pot of what's filtered on through.

Young people on the Tulse Hill estate in Brixton, where I lived, came to the rescue as my dialogue consultants. The over-smart 'slangstas' at Lambeth's *Live Magazine* ("by young peeps, for young peeps") helped out too. These 12-21-year-olds advised me on what's current, while warning me about slang's in-built obsolescence factor. Once I'd got a feel for the rhythms and resonances of slang in South London, its colour, mood and humour, my task was to engineer an equivalent: but preferably with a longer shelf-life. As the Mexican writer, Carlos Fuentes, remarked when delivering the 2004 NESTA Max Sebald Lecture at London's South Bank Centre: "Translators can't convey the slang of our times accurately, because slang is language in constant transformation. So we have to give slang an 'onomatopoeic resonance' by transforming language into comical expression."

Consulting with these young people about the stories they wanted to read from other countries, creating the kind of dialogue they felt was an accurate portrayal of how their contemporaries might talk if they were dubbed into English, are what most inspired my extended sense of the translator as go-between, observer and writer. From the Algerian rappers who wowed me with their (at first) incoherent *verlan* in Marseille, to the UK street slangstas who talked a whole new language, I relished forging encounters between words and people, as well as witnessing so-called non-linguists offering up fiery translations of their own. Now that really is a case of monsters growing arms and legs. From my perspective, it ain't what you lose but *how you gain it* in translation.

Everyday Miracles

Lene Kaaberbol

Some UK bookshops have sections labelled: 'Literature in Translation'. As if translations need their own little reservation, sheltered and protected, sought out only by academics with a taste for the unusual.

Please. Don't put me in that reservation.

I have no wish to be sheltered. I do not want to be labelled as unusual. I just want to write, and be read, in as many languages as I can manage. So far, I am indecorously proud to say, my work has been translated into more than twenty languages of quite stunning diversity – Japanese, Cantonese, Finnish, Inuit, Hungarian, Turkish and Latvian, to name but a few. I don't think that my readers in those faraway places have paid any attention whatsoever to the fact that they were reading a translated work. What they have heard, I hope, is the voice of Dina, the Shamer's daughter, speaking to them in their native tongue with naturalness and authority, sweeping them into her world and her story. After all, no author sets out to create Literature in Translation. Most of us just write a book.

In Denmark, where I live, a 'Literature In Translation' section would be completely nonsensical – it would comprise more than half the shop. In a small country like ours, a book is a book, whether translated or home-grown, which is as it should be.

It is a thrill and a privilege to be translated, but a pleasure shot through with threads of paranoia. True translation, in the strictest sense, is impossible. How can you separate a story from the words that make it up? It is like separating the soul from the body. I think I share with every translated author those little moments of panic: "My God, I've given them my baby, and they've made it speak Japanese! What have they done to it? I wouldn't even recognise it if it weren't for my pathetic little photo on the flap!" Yet at the same time, I get an immense kick out of knowing that there are children in this world who read my books from the back, moving their eyes up and down the page, rather than across.

If we wish to cross borders, we must also cross language barriers. So we send our stories off, like Hansel and Gretel, to find a way through the wilderness, hoping not too much will be lost along the way. Occasionally, a few breadcrumbs are tossed, in the shape of letters or phone calls from translators, asking questions, seeking reassurance that they are on the right track. At other times, there is merely silence. Right, you tell yourself. Surely this means that everything is going just fine, your story and the translator have met and are getting on famously, a successful language transplant is expected any day now . . .

And the miracle is that this is usually the case. By the grace of your translator, through her talent, hard labour and dedication, your story is about to be reincarnated: born fresh in a language you yourself cannot even read, let alone write. A necessary, everyday miracle that opens the gate to a wider world.

But please – let those little miracles off the reservation. They do not want to be treated like incubated marvels, pampered and cosseted, kept from the real world. They want to come out and play with the other children.

When it comes to the English version of my work, I am in the unusual position of being both the author and the translator. No longer am I doomed to watch from the wings, caught between dumb gratitude and neurotic paranoia. This time, I get to speak the lines myself. And I have one enormous advantage over most translators: I can cheat. If something doesn't work, I can simply change it. So far, the author hasn't complained . . .

Thus, translation for me isn't really translation, but rather one more rewrite. There is a peculiar freedom in moving from one language to another. I find that I see the story afresh. Habitual assumptions drop by the wayside, and not all of those assumptions are to do with linguistics. I've been able to work out knots in the plot by shifting languages. I've gained new insight into what my characters might say and do. Translation for me has become a writer's tool, a way to switch lenses; a way of seeing.

On the face of it, this makes no sense at all. Why should the story assume a different shape to me, just because I'm writing it in English? Yet it does – because language is not just a range of sounds and signs we use to communicate with other human beings. Language is bound up with the way we see the world. And despite teasing similarities, even the most closely related of languages do not match, word for word. A switch in language means a switch in perception.

Or, as Edith Grossman puts it: "a translation is not made with tracing paper. It is an act of critical interpretation. Let me insist on the obvious: Languages trail immense, individual histories behind them, and no two languages, with all their accretions of tradition and culture, ever dovetail perfectly". And who is Edith Grossman? Though they have enjoyed her words, probably not many of her readers remember her name. She is the translator of one of today's greatest living writers, Gabriel

Garcia Marquez. He is lucky to have her, and I think he knows it.

A story by Gabriel Garcia Marquez will never be an English story, no matter how excellently translated. It will be something much better: a story that has made a miraculous transformation, a second incarnation which holds still the unique flavours, scents, and sounds of its original Colombian-Spanish soul.

Translation is impossible. Transformation is not. Praise be to the unsung heroes who perform such miracles.

Oh, and please . . . let them off the reservation.

Edith Grossman's speech at the PEN Gabriel Garcia Marquez tribute (2003) may be read in its entirety at http://www.themodernword.com/gabo/gabo_PEN_grossman.html

Discovering difference: studying translations for children at Roehampton

Gillian Lathey

At the beginning of the 1990s, Kim Reynolds and Pat Pinsent began to put together a range of exciting courses to form a new Children's Literature MA at Roehampton University. Seizing the opportunity to develop a keen and long-standing interest in both children's literature and translation, I offered a module on Children's Literature in Translation that would, I hoped, introduce students to the work of the best writers for children across the world and to the skills and artistry of those 'unsung heroes' (Michael Ignatieff), the translators. We started small, of course; I can recall four of us sitting round a table and learning from one participant, Tomoko Masaki, that a translated Japanese picture book which appeared to be a joyous account of a birthday party, was in the original quite a tragic little tale – a stark instance not of translation, but of editorial invention of a text to fit the pictures in a British publishing house.

Tomoko's revelation was only the first of many memorable contributions from MA students that have highlighted both the role of translation and cross-cultural influences in the international history of children's literatures. Overseas students come into their own on this course, both as experts in their own national children's literatures and as bi- or multilingual speakers of languages other than English. British students have listened spellbound to accounts of the subversive role of the Greek children's literature during the Turkish occupation, when it was taught secretly in church crypts; of the fragile development of an indigenous children's literature in the Philippines through successive waves of colonisation; of the emergence of graphic novels for young adults in Taiwan and the equivalent manga tradition in Japan. Student seminar presentations like these are the starting point for essays, several of which have reached publishable standard. Students have also generously enriched resources by donating books in original languages (*Pinocchio* in Italian and *Pippi Longstocking* in Swedish) or out-of-print translations – the marvellous *Papa Pellerin's Daughter* by Maria Gripe and *The Satanic Mill* by Otfried Preussler are now available to future students by this route.

So what actually happens on those dark winter evenings at Roehampton in the translation class? We begin by comparing different translations into English of stories with which all students are familiar: Perrault's *Cendrillon* (Cinderella), the Grimm Brothers' *Aschenputtel*, or *Pinocchio*. It is not necessary to know the language of the original – indeed, the course was originally designed for monolingual English speakers – but, whenever possible, access to source languages adds a further dimension to discussion. What gradually emerges through comparison of source and target-language texts is evidence of what Theo Hermans (1996) has called the translator's 'discursive presence'. Translation doesn't just happen in a straightforward word-for-word manner: there is clearly a filtering consciousness at work making linguistic choices, adapting the context of the original, aligning it with models in the receiving culture, omitting text or adding explanations. Close textual analysis and comparison also tease out requirements unique to translating for children – an appreciation of read-aloud qualities in stories for the very young, or of the role of the visual in picture books and the 'bande dessinée'.

Both the many variants of the Cinderella story and translations of Pinocchio illustrate the impact of didacticism, or of changing notions of what is good for the child, on the translation process. Censorship leads to the complete omission of any mutilation of the sisters' heels and toes in translations for a child readership of *Aschenputtel*, although some translators merely tone down such gruesome passages. And in a familiar pattern of context adaptation that often underestimates the child reader's ability to engage with the unfamiliar, the Oxford World Classics edition of 1996 replaces Italian dishes with shepherd's pie and steak and kidney pudding. To bring such discussion up to date, seminars on the Harry Potter series in recent years reveal the speed and effectiveness of global marketing, with translators under pressure as never before as each new title appears. A close reading of the first chapter of *Harry Potter and the Philosopher's Stone*, with students bringing along translations into their native languages has initiated debates on the translation of Rowling's playfully ironic and colloquial tone; on how to convey the 'Britishness' of a text that relies on a knowledge of boarding school traditions and, more specifically, on translating the non-standard English spoken by Hagrid. Even the opening line of chapter one presents the translator with a challenge: how to render the address 'number four, Privet Drive', resonant with suggestions of suburban conformity and neatly-mown lawns, in the target language?

A second, but equally significant, strand to the module is the literary content and form of children's texts from across the world. A rediscovery of *Pinocchio*, for example, establishes Collodi's satirical intent, the story's impact as a linguistic and literary icon in Italy and its position alongside *Peter Pan*, *Alice* and *Pippi Longstocking* as one of the great children's texts about the paradoxes of growing up. Landmark children's authors of

the twentieth century Erich Kästner and Astrid Lindgren also appear on the syllabus. No-one has understood or written for the five-to-twelve-year-old better than Lindgren. The pace, intensity and rhythmic language of the fairytale fantasy novels *Mio my Mio*, *The Brothers Lionheart* and *Ronia the Robber's Daughter* are her greatest achievements and, sadly, little known in the UK. Finally, two sessions on British and translated literature on the Second World War allow for enlightening comparison of texts that tell different sides of that particular story.

That leaves just a little time for poetry, the hardest translation task of all, and for discussion of recent translated publications that cause students to re-think the notion of difference in the form and content of children's books. Hans Magnus Enzensberger's *Where Were You Robert?* or Jostein Gaarder's *Sophie's World* signal an intellectual edge to continental European fiction, while the hard-hitting political writing of Anne Provoost's *Falling*, or the powerfully elliptical domestic dramas of Bart Moeyaert's *Bare Hands* are examples of an impressive wave of new realism in Belgian novels for young adults. Fortunately, the course has always evolved to accommodate both the cultural histories of participants, and the welcome increase in the publication of translations. Translated books appear on the reading lists of undergraduate sessions at Roehampton, too, and there are plans to include children's literature as a specialist option on a new Translation MA. From the array of academic dissertations and essays generated by the course, to the comment of a graduating MA student that she now looks out for translated books and makes a point of giving one to her children at Christmas, there is plenty to suggest that studying translations for children opens minds and leads to unpredictable discoveries.

Squiggles and Dots: Bilingual Books for Children

Patricia Billings

Faced with new and seemingly strange texts, children don't turn away: they look. They ask: what does this mean? Can a stream of what looks like squiggles and dots actually say something? Bit by bit, they learn that it does, that the stream of unfamiliar letters or characters is imbued with rich meanings, as well as visual beauty. They may not understand every letter, word or character, but they have begun to understand and appreciate a new language – the strange is demystified, normalized, embraced.

While Britain is often bemoaned as a monolingual nation, voices on the ground speak differently. There are no firm statistics on how many people in Britain are bilingual, but a recent study reported that more than 300 different languages are spoken in London alone, and that one third of London school-children speak a language other than English at home. While the big cities will have the greater share of bilinguals, most corners of Britain are now host to many language groups. Despite the sometimes unhelpful discourse on 'home' languages emanating from officials, in schools, homes, offices, and on the streets, bilingualism in Britain is thriving.

Old anxieties about bilingualism in children, fears that the speaking and reading of home languages would interfere with the learning of English, gave way as the science of language acquisition in the young showed that the young mind is eminently capable of, and indeed ideally suited for acquiring multiple languages; that the skills used to learn one language can be readily transferred to other languages; and that these skills have overall cognitive benefits for the child, even beyond the realm of language. On the social level, as the recognition of the benefits of multi-culturalism has increased over time, so too has the appreciation of the value of languages, including the retaining of home languages, of learning new languages and of being bilingual.

Likewise, corresponding myths that surrounded bilingual books in their early days were soon debunked. The belief that children brought up with English would always focus on English when reading bilingual books because it was the 'easier' language was dismissed by studies showing that the child attempts to read both languages. The understanding that multiple languages complement rather than compete with each other helped to allay worries among parents of bilingual children that the study or active use of their home language would adversely affect their learning of English.

The first generation of bilingual books, though groundbreaking and valuable, might be seen as tending toward the worthy, covering titles and themes that were explicitly multicultural and with varying production quality. More recent waves of bilingual books, more confident in their purpose and their ability to grasp a larger market, have broadened thematically, choosing stories as much for their narrative and visual pleasures as for their meanings. These books have excelled in design and production quality as well, recognizing that readers of languages other than English deserve the same high standard books as readers of English. So bilingual books are beautiful, engaging and innovative; they encompass everything from story books to picture dictionaries to flap books to multi-media materials.

Young readers, their parents, carers and educators now have a rich variety of materials to choose from in a broad range of languages, from more commonly learned European languages like French and Italian, to the languages of the country's largest bilingual communities, like Bengali, Urdu, Chinese and Turkish, to those spoken by smaller groups, such as Serbo-Croatian and Dinka.

And bilingual books can be read and enjoyed by all: they can help bilingual children raised here to develop literacy skills in their home languages; for newly-arrived immigrant and refugee families, the books can be crucial aids for developing literacy in English, and for inclusion in reading at school and at home; they are important and enjoyable learning aids, as well, for English-speaking children learning other languages, used on their own or alongside textbooks; and even for those not yet learning another language, they provide an ideal introduction to the wealth of languages and scripts in the world, helping to inspire interest in other languages, and in other cultures and countries.

Bilingual books are available for all age ranges, with the greatest number of titles aimed at the pre-school and primary levels. There are far fewer titles for older children and teenagers, reflecting an assumption (not necessarily correct) that children from other language groups will have learned English by the secondary education stage. Also, for publishers, longer texts are more costly and difficult to produce in dual-language, so, with an uncertain market, they can be hesitant, but there is hope that the range of materials for this age group will grow.

Indeed, publishers of bilingual books face many challenges. The publisher must choose titles that translate smoothly cross-culturally. They must investigate the languages in current demand – the pool of languages is constantly changing, based often on political events and their associated migrations. When translating, publishers must consider different dialects and scripts, and how far to go in innovating with the translation, rather than adhering strictly to the original English text (my publishing company has favoured innovation). The dual-language publisher must be attuned to cultural sensitivities when considering the text and pictures, as many different cultural groups will be addressed at the same time in one print run of multiple language editions. Text design in the books is more complicated, as it must accommodate and respect more than one language. There are the additional printing costs for running many languages, then special research and efforts are required to market and distribute the books to their target language groups.

Bilingual publishing is intensive on all levels, so it may not be attractive to all publishers. But it has certainly proved attractive to some publishers: Britain boasts a large, diverse and growing selection of bilingual books which offer eye-opening experiences, learning opportunities and, not the least, pleasures and delights to young readers.

A Publisher's Perspective

Klaus Flugge

I have published translations of children's books ever since I came to Britain in 1961 as publisher of Abelard-Schuman and, since 1976 when I founded Andersen Press, which I had the cheek to name after the greatest writer of children's stories on the Continent. However, the 60s saw many more translated books thanks to the support of the librarians who spent much more money on children's books than they are able to do now.

The general public still seems reluctant to buy books by authors with names that are difficult to pronounce. Maybe that's the reason why Christine Nöstlinger never became very popular in Britain, unlike any other country. She was the first winner of the *Astrid Lindgren Memorial Award* (worth almost £400,000, awarded by the Swedish Government).

It took quite a few years for the books about a loveable Frog by Max Velthuijs to become popular in Britain. Our former sales director used to ask me to change his name to Fieldhouse if I wanted to increase my sales.

'the 60s saw many more translated books thanks to the support of the librarians'

There are of course other reasons for the shortage of translated books: the amazing number of children's books written in English, the reluctance of editors to take in books they can't read themselves and the now considerable cost of translation. Quite a few European countries used to underwrite this but budgets for such support have been cut considerably over the last couple of years.

This year Andersen Press will have published three translations, not enough, but already more than most other children's publishers. I very much hope that this excellent catalogue will increase awareness of and interest in the life and literature of other countries.

The Story of WingedChariot

Neal Hoskins

As a small publisher starting out, I suppose more than anything your choice of books really comes down to gut feeling. There I was in Amsterdam in 2004 with a free day before a talk I was going to give to the Dutch Reading Association, and as often happens, my meandering led me to a bookshop where I picked up a little book called *Drop* – which means literally something like, but much more than, our home grown Liquorice Allsorts. Unknown to me then, *Drop* was to become the book that a year later started our list of European picture books. With the added assistance of a grant from Arts Council England we set about publishing four books, two from the Netherlands and two from Portugal. In addition to these titles we also wanted to do something extra. We knew that librarians and teachers, as well as parents, would enjoy these books so together with our editor, Ann Arscott, we started work on introductory booklets for the titles and recorded the stories in the original languages. We loved the sound of these different languages, and thought the books would be a good way in which to introduce the idea of Europe and other cross-cultural discussions, especially with the internet now as an additional means of delivery.

The greatest challenge for these books will be to find their feet in the British picture book market. I do not know what it is about European books that make them slightly different – perhaps they are somehow more open, more extreme or louder than the English ones; perhaps in the end they take a more philosophical viewpoint on life. The mass market for picture books is often the funny endearing bedtime stories that everyone loves reading with kids. But the books we want to publish, and which in turn help us stand out, can be enjoyed by all ages. We know the time is right for an injection of new talent and new stories with different perspectives on life around us.

We have carefully crafted our books – stitching and varnishing the covers – and have worked on every one as an individual project. On our poetry title we approached a well-known poet to work on an English version as we felt we wanted to keep the rhymes. It was a risk and hard to do taking more time than planned but we think it has worked superbly. Our view on translation is that we are always trying to find the right voice for the books even if there are only 50 words inside, and we are happy to work with translators and established writers where necessary to write the best English version of the story. Some of our inspiration came from the layout of Brian Wildsmith's illustrations of Robert Louis Stevenson's *A Child's Garden of Verse* done in the 60s, simplifying the covers leaving just the title and pictures.

The reaction to previews of the books from the public and the trade has been wonderful. We know we have to be realistic and in order for the imprint to survive, our books must stand out and stand up for themselves in a competitive market - something different, something magnificent for people to enjoy. Our first four titles are contained in this guide. We plan to publish another six books from Germany, France and Finland, the latter being something of a publishing first as was the case with our Portuguese titles.

The great Max Velthuijs, author of the wonderful Frog books, once said he only became an illustrator for children's books because no other publisher wanted them in their adult list of titles – who knows what other ventures and new possibilities lie ahead for us in the more distant future . . .

Babar has come to England: Classic European Children's Literature in Translation

Edgardo Zaghini

Children's literature in translation enriches our lives because it provides a glimpse into the experiences and way of life of children from different parts of the world. It offers the opportunity to travel, in our imagination, to far away places and to learn about other cultures. The tradition of translating literature for children has a long history, particularly in Europe, and this article will show some of the major contributions that they have made.

Germany has provided us with outstanding classic works of literature. *The Nutcracker* by E.T.A. Hoffman first appeared in German in 1816 – a story about nursery toys battling against a mouse army and the Nutcracker prince who has been enchanted by a mouse sorcerer. One of the best editions so far is the one illustrated by Italian artist, Roberto Innocenti. The Fairy Tales of the brothers Grimm are some of the best-known tales in translation – *Rapunzel*, *The Frog Prince*, *Hansel and Gretel*, *Rumpelstiltskin* are just a few of the tales which started to appear in the German language from 1822. Since then there have been innumerable collections and editions of Grimm fairy tales in many languages. *Struwwelpeter*, by Dr Heinrich Hoffmann, was first published in translation in 1848. It is a cautionary tale, highly educational and moralistic in content and with gruesome illustrations that caused uproar among contemporary readers at the time. Wilhelm Busch's *Max and Moritz* (1865), a comic poem about two young pranksters who play tricks on the village people, can be considered the ancestor of modern comics.

Erich Kästner gave birth to one of the most memorable stories ever written in the twentieth century, *Emil and the Detectives* (1929). It was translated into English in 1931 with an introduction by Walter de la Mare and black-and-white line drawings by Walter Trier. It depicts the adventures of a gang of children in Berlin trying to catch a thief. If you ever want to be transported to that city during the 1920s, then this book will do the trick. Other titles by Kästner that have been translated into English are *Emil and the Three Twins*, *The Flying Classroom* (1934), a school adventure story for boys and *Lottie and Lisa* (1949). However, none of these reached the colossal international success that *Emil and the Detectives* did. One of the most talented artists of the twentieth century also came from Germany: Janosch (real name Horst Eckert, born in Poland in 1931); his book *The Big Janosch Book of Fun and Verse* came out in 1980.

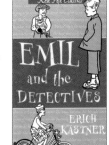

Switzerland produced the now well-known tale of a young orphan living in the Alps with her grandfather. *Heidi* by Johanna Spyri was first published in 1880 and later translated into English from German. Its continued popularity has inspired many films and television versions. There have been two sequels written by Charles Tritten, *Heidi Grows Up* (1961) and *Heidi's Children* (1967). *The Swiss Family Robinson* by J. D. Wyss is another novel to emerge from this country. It was first published in 1812 and tells the story of a family shipwrecked on a desert island. It was translated two years after its publication and there have been more than three hundred different editions published in England and America alone.

Although born in Vienna, Vojtech Kubasta can be considered a Czech citizen, as it was in Prague that he built an amazing careēr as artist, designer and paper engineer and his reputation in this field has not yet been surpassed. Kubasta's movable books have been crossing international borders even during those dangerous years of communism when he was commissioned to work for international companies. His panoramic books are highly sought after by collectors today; *How Columbus Discovered America* and *Moko and Koko in the Jungle* are just two examples of his incredible workmanship.

France's contribution to children's literature has been remarkable. The Fables of La Fontaine were published between 1668 and 1694 and they were largely based on Aesop's Fables. It took a long time for these fables to appear in English and it was in 1734 that they were finally translated. Perrault was the genius who collected the fairy stories of *Little Red Riding Hood*, *Cinderella* and *The Sleeping Beauty* to mention just a few of the most popular ones, and they have continued to appear in many volumes and formats since 1696. *The Three Musketeers* (1844) by Alexandre Dumas and Jules Verne's *Twenty Thousand Leagues under the Sea* (1870) were both considered classics of children's literature prior to the 1970s, although today they are more likely to appeal to young readers in an abridged format. Verne also wrote *Around the World in Eighty Days* (1873), the story of Phileas Fogg who vowed to make his way across the globe in a mere eighty days. This book has succeeded in depicting cultures as diverse as Victorian England, Colonial India and the American Wild West.

Jean de Brunhoff's little elephant *Babar* enjoys as much popularity today as when the books were first published back in the 1930s. The first seven Babar stories were published between the years 1931 and 1937, all depicting the well-known eponymous hero dressed in a green suit and gold crown. The big format, bold colour, double-page spread and hand-written text made a generous contribution to the development of picture books at the time.

René Guillot was another French children's author of over fifty novels who specialised in adventure stories, many of them translated into English. His most popular book was *Companion of Fortune* (1952). *The Little Prince* (1943) by Antoine de Saint-Exupéry is an allegorical exploration of the human condition. *Asterix*, a Gaul who lives in a village in Brittany, the last holdout against the Romans, is the ultimate French comic hero created by René Goscinny (text) and Albert Uderzo (illustrations), and first appeared in the comic weekly *Pilote* in 1959. Paul Hazard has always been regarded as the father of French children's literature and his classic *Books, Children and Men: a Survey of Children's Literature in Europe* was first published in English in 1944. It has been a valuable reference source ever since.

Belgium has produced a classic comic hero of its own the famous teenage reporter *Tintin* by Hergé, who gets involved in all kinds of thrilling adventures. Tintin first appeared in comic serials in 1929 and started to appear in the UK from 1958. The *Spike and Suzy* series created by Willy Vandersteen are delightful comics that were originally published in Belgium over fifty years ago and are still in

Classics

print today, having sold millions of copies and translated into over twenty different languages all over the world. The Belgian author Morris is best known for his humorous cowboy character, *Lucky Luke*. The first episode was published in *L'Almanach Spirou* in 1947 and the series is still one of the most popular in European comic history.

From the Netherlands comes the moving and touching true story of a young girl's thoughts, aspirations and observations of daily life while hiding in the secret annexe of a flat in Nazi-occupied Amsterdam during the Second World War. *The Diary of Anne Frank* was first published in 1947 and since then has been translated into over fifty languages and is today a symbol of the racial hatred and xenophobia that have marked a shameful period in European history.

Cuore (Heart) by Italian author Edmondo de Amicis, a former professional soldier, was written in the aftermath of the Italian war for independence and the unification of Italy in 1870. It was published in 1886 at a time when Italy was beginning to enjoy her newly won unity and is the fictional diary of a young boy's life in a Turin school. The intention of the book was to foster an appreciation of national identity and it has become required reading for generations of Italians up to the present day. The first English translation appeared in 1903 and it has subsequently been translated into twenty-five different languages, adapted for film, television, radio, plays and comic books.

The other classic is the well-known tale of *Pinocchio* by Carlo Collodi. It was originally written for a Rome children's magazine, the *Giornale dei bambini*, and only appeared in book format in 1883. *Pinocchio* was first translated into English in 1892 and there have been numerous translations and adaptations into English ever since. As well as having been translated into many other languages throughout the world *Pinocchio* also became internationally recognised when Walt Disney made a film of it in 1940. Works by other more contemporary authors translated into English are Italo Calvino's *Italian Folktales* and Gianni Rodari's *Telephone Tales*, originally translated into English in 1965.

From Spain comes *Marcelino, Pan y Vino* (*Marcelino, Bread and Wine*, sometimes known as *The Miracle of Marcelino* or *Adventures in Heaven of Marcelino*) by Jose Maria Sanchez-Silva, published in 1952. It is a tale of an orphan boy, who is adopted by monks, and finds that early death, however sad, means a joyous entry into paradise. Besides this highly religious message, Marcelino represents the normal virtues and vices of a nine-year-old Spanish boy.

The Scandinavian countries have been remarkable in the production of literature for children and the UK has translated many of their treasures. From Finland comes *The Moomins* by Tove Jansson. These stories about Moomin Valley, a fantastic place full of magic and mystery, have been in print in this country since the early 1950s. The first book, *The Little Trolls and the Great Flood* (1945) was never published in Britain, but all the subsequent eleven have been. From Norway comes the hilarious *Mrs Pepperpot* series by Alf Prøysen. Mrs Pepperpot has the ability to shrink to the size of a pepperpot at the most convenient moment. These books first appeared in the UK in 1959.

From Denmark come the fairy tales of Hans Christian Andersen, their most famous author, who has achieved recognition throughout the world. Andersen's stories first appear in English in 1846 and there have been numerous translations and retellings ever since. *I am David* (1963) is a touching novel by Danish writer Anne Holm about a boy escaping from a concentration camp in an unnamed Eastern bloc country. The first English translation appeared in 1965.

From Sweden comes *The Wonderful Adventures of Nils* (1906-7) by Selma Lagerlöf, the famous story

of a Tom-Thumb-like being who can communicate with animals. Last but not least is the critically acclaimed Swedish author of *Pippi Longstocking* (1945), Astrid Lindgren. Pippi is her most enduring character and it is the story of the strongest girl in the world who lives alone in Villekulla Cottage, with only a horse and a monkey for company. Many of Lindgren's children's books have been translated into English and the prestigious international *Astrid Lingdren Memorial Award* is named after her.

There has always been a long-standing tradition of children's literature in translation in other countries, but, alas, the same tradition has not been consistently evident in Britain. There are a small number of publishers reissuing classics as can be seen from the bibliography, but much more could be done. We should recognise the contribution made to children's literature by the world's authors and join other countries in their passion for sharing stories and authors from other cultures.

Bibliography

Around the World in Eighty Days, Jules Verne, Puffin Books (2004)
PB £6.99 ISBN: 014062032X

Asterix books by René Goscinny, Orion Children's Books. Books 1–15 of the Asterix titles are available. Asterix and the Cauldron (Book 13), Asterix in Spain (Book 14) and Asterix and the Roman Agent (Book 15) are the most recent titles.

Babar Books by L. de Brunhoff, Harry N. Abrams (USA) whole range of titles available.

The Book about Moomin, Mymble and Little My Tove Jansson, translated by Sophie Hannah Sort of Books (2001) HB ISBN: 0953522741

Cuore (The Heart of a Boy) Edmondo de Amicis, translated by Desmond Hartley, Peter Owen Publishers (2005) PB £9.95 ISBN: 0720612322

The Diary of a Young Girl Anne Frank, translated by Susan Massotty, Puffin Books (2002) PB £6.99 ISBN: 0141315180
(there are a whole range of Anne Frank titles available in print)

Emil and the Detectives Erich Kästner, illustrated by Walter Trier, Red Fox (2001) PB £5.99 ISBN: 0099413124

Emil and the Three Twins Erich Kästner, illustrated by Walter Trier, Red Fox (2002) PB £4.99 ISBN: 09943363X

Finn Family Moomintroll Tove Jansson, translated by Elizabeth Portch, Puffin Books (2004) PB £4.99 ISBN: 014030150X (another five titles are still available)

Hans Christian Andersen
(there are many different collections of his stories available in print)

Heidi Johanna Spyri, Penguin Books (2004) PB ISBN: 0140621911

The Little Prince Antoine de Saint-Exupéry, Egmont Children's Books (2000) PB £9.99 ISBN: 0749743859

The Nutcracker E.T.A. Hoffman, illustrated by Roberto Innocenti, Creative Editions (2005) HB ISBN: 151002274

Mrs Pepperpot Collection Alf Prøysen, Red Fox (2000) PB £5.99 ISBN: 0099411393 (other titles are due to be reissued)

Pinocchio Carlo Collodi, illustrated by Roberto Innocenti, Jonathan Cape (2005) HB £14.99 ISBN: 0224070568

Pippi Longstocking Astrid Lindgren, illustrated by Tony Ross, Oxford University Press (2002) PB £4.99 ISBN: 0192752049 (*Pippi in the South Seas* and *Pippi Goes Abroad* are also available from OUP)

Spike and Suzy and the Loch Ness Mystery (Vol 5) 1999 (available from wwwmilehighcomics.com)

The Swiss Family Robinson Johann David Wyss, Dodo P (2005) PB ISBN: 190543250X

Tintin books by Hergé, Egmont Children's Books have a whole range of titles available including *The Tintin and Alph-Art* (2004) £9.99 ISBN: 1405214481

The Three Musketeers Alexandre Dumas, translated by Lord Sudley, Penguin Books (1982) PB ISBN: 0140440259

Twenty Thousand Leagues Under the Sea Jules Verne, translated by William Butcher, Oxford University Press (1998) PB £6.99 ISBN: 0192828398

The Wonderful Adventures of Nils Selma Lagerlöf, illustrated by Lars Klinting, Floris Books (2001) HB £11.99 ISBN: 0863151396

Pablo Bernasconi

was born in 1973, in Buenos Aires, Argentina. He graduated from the Universidad de Buenos Aires as a graphic designer, where he later taught design for over six years. Pablo began his career as an illustrator in 1998 with the *Clarín* newspaper in Argentina where he designed covers for over 200 editions. His work has also been published in other major international newspapers. Pablo has won three awards of excellence (in 2001, 2002 and 2004) from the Society of New Design for art and illustration, individual portfolio and cover design, for *Clarín* (Argentina) and *La vox de Galicia* (Spain) newspapers. He was also selected to participate in Lurzer's Archive 200 Best Illustrators Worldwide.

Pablo has written and illustrated several children's books: *Black Skin, White Cow* (2004) and *Hippos Can Swim* (2005) for Random House, Australia, *Captain Arsenio's Diary* (2005) for Houghton Mifflin, America and *The Wizard, the Ugly and the Book of Shame* which is his first book to be published in the UK by Bloomsbury Children's Books and is featured in this guide on page 51.

'My experience with translated books was first as a reader, and then as an author. I am extremely grateful to literature in translation for the way it has influenced me. This huge cultural influence has surely meant much more than just some texts to have fun with. I learned so much from them, I understood the directions and trends of children's books abroad, and could apply it to my own local projects.

It is a great feeling to be read by children from so far away, of so many different cultures, yet still keep the essence of the book. It is great to reach the mind of a child and to feel so close'

Blue & Square
Hervé Tullet

Translated from French
Milet Publishing (2002) HB £4.99
ISBN: 1 84059 343 1

Yellow & Round
Hervé Tullet

Translated from French
Milet Publishing (2002) HB £4.99
ISBN: 1 84059 344 X

Here are two very original board books by Hervé Tullet featuring simple and important opposites. Each book has a die-cut – square in *Blue & Square* or circle in *Yellow & Round* – at its core that children can play with on every page. In *Blue & Square* opposites like inside and outside, big and small and sad and happy are used, while in *Yellow & Round* above and below, clean and dirty and near and far are featured. These concepts are illustrated with bold, vibrant colours and the books are beautifully produced and especially sturdy for repeated use.

Night and Day
Hervé Tullet

Translated from French
Milet Publishing (1999) HB £8.99
ISBN: 1 84059 111 0

Pink Lemon
Hervé Tullet

Translated from French
Milet Publishing (2001) HB £8.99
ISBN: 1 84059 330 X

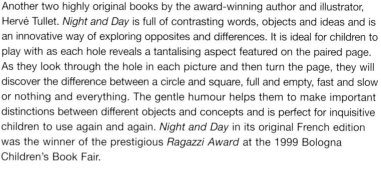

Another two highly original books by the award-winning author and illustrator, Hervé Tullet. *Night and Day* is full of contrasting words, objects and ideas and is an innovative way of exploring opposites and differences. It is ideal for children to play with as each hole reveals a tantalising aspect featured on the paired page. As they look through the hole in each picture and then turn the page, they will discover the difference between a circle and square, full and empty, fast and slow or nothing and everything. The gentle humour helps them to make important distinctions between different objects and concepts and is perfect for inquisitive children to use again and again. *Night and Day* in its original French edition was the winner of the prestigious *Ragazzi Award* at the 1999 Bologna Children's Book Fair.

Pink Lemon is a playful book about colours. Each spread shows a picture of an object, but is it the right colour? Children will love the pictures of a green sun, black toothpaste, a blue orange, yellow sea and a pink lemon and they will learn by choosing the correct colour for each. This is a book to inspire a child's imagination and encourage them to experiment with colours and perception. Parents can have great fun using this book together with their children.

Dear Grandma Bunny
Dick Bruna

Translated from Dutch by Patricia Crampton
Egmont Children's Books (2005) HB £3.99
ISBN: 1 4052 1901 7

Miffy's Garden
Dick Bruna

Translated from Dutch by Patricia Crampton
Egmont Children's Books (2005) HB £3.99
ISBN: 1 4052 1902 5

Two of three new titles in Miffy's Classic Story Library published to celebrate 50 years of Miffy stories. Together with *Miffy and the New Baby*, in which Miffy comes to terms with the idea of a new sibling, these books deal with sensitive issues in a child's life. In *Miffy's Garden* the little rabbit discovers how satisfying hard work can be, and the rewards it brings. *Dear Grandma Bunny* introduces that most difficult subject of all: the death of a loved one. In this story Miffy joins in the grief, the ceremonial and the celebrations that commemorate Grandma Bunny herself and her contribution to the extended family. Dick Bruna's illustrations perfectly catch the intensity of emotion experienced by young children, and the familiar rhymed translation provides a memorable text for listening to and joining in. Bruna does not shirk the physical aspects of death, and portrays Grandma Bunny, unusually still, but clearly peaceful. Excellent additions to the library of lovely little books about this universally loved character.

Merry Christmas – a Superdog Adventure
Raphaël Thierry

Translated from French by
Raphaël Thierry and Jeffrey Paul Kearney
Andersen Press (2004) PB £4.99
ISBN: 1 84270 419 2

Green Butterfly – a Superdog Adventure
Raphaël Thierry

Translated from French by
Raphaël Thierry and Jeffrey Paul Kearney
Andersen Press (2005) PB £4.99
ISBN: 1 84270 449 4

Characterised by their use of variations on a bold base colour for cover and spreads (*Merry Christmas* is in leaf greens, *Green Butterfly* in dusky pinks), and by the covers extending into flaps, these are highly attractive little picture books with splendidly minimalist illustration, and a very enterprising dog as protagonist. *Green Butterfly* was the first in the series of picture books about Superdog, a deceptively simple four-footed philosopher. In this adventure a little butterfly passes Superdog, and comments that he is still attached to his post, while it is free as the air. But Superdog is very inventive, and he manages to turn all the way upside down too, even though he is tied up – and he can see . . . nearly everything. He is concentrating so hard on his acrobatics that he doesn't spot the butterfly fluttering off. In the second book, Superdog is promised he'll receive a present for Christmas, and tries to think what it could be. The parcel arrives and it's a pair of scissors. He snips himself free but soon he's back, because, after all, Superdog is too attached to his post. A delightful way for children to ponder the expectation that presents engender, before they realise that sometimes what you already have is better than what you desire. Still to be published are four further titles in which Superdog discovers the world which surrounds him, and how to cope with it.

Tiger on a Tree

Anushka Ravishankar, illustrated by Pulak Biswas

Tara Publications (2002) HB £9.99
ISBN: 81 86211 35 7

This is a story about a wild tiger cub that wanders into a village looking for adventure on the shores of a river. Suddenly, he is scared by a goat and looks for refuge in a tree. He is discovered by a group of villagers who are frightened and decide to capture him. They surround the tree and with the help of a net Tiger is trapped. Now they have to decide what to do with him! *Tiger on a Tree* is an internationally award-winning book written in Indian/English nonsense verse. The story has a charming simplicity with light verse spreading in waves through the pages. Full of rhythm and onomatopoeic words, this is a wonderful story to read aloud. Pulak Biswas' simplistic hand silk-screened illustrations complement the narrative with the use of the two colours, ("tigerish" black and orange, across white hand-made paper) and bring alive the expressive characters from one of India's best children's book illustrators.

My Friend

Beatrice Alemagna

Translated from French
North-South Books (2005) HB £9.99 ISBN: 0 7358 1993 9

A very unusual creature that has fur like a dog and is shaped like a sheep doesn't know what he is. As he goes on his way, he encounters a multitude of people and animals, each one interpreting his identity differently – he isn't a pigeon, a lion, crocodile or even a hippopotamus – but no one getting it right. When he meets an equally unusual animal they both accept each other as friends without questioning their being or where they came from. It would be nice to see more of this type of picture book published in the UK with its highly innovative, clever and original story and illustrations by Beatrice Alemagna. It also conveys an important international message of accepting people beyond their colour, nationality or appearance and of reassuring any child that feels different. The illustrations are stunning: collage type artwork, using a variety of textiles, buttons and threads in double spread pages that perfectly depict different feelings and emotions.

Will Gets a Haircut

Olof and Lena Landström

Translated from Swedish by Elisabeth Kallick Dyssegaard
R&S Books (2000) PB £3.99 ISBN: 91 29 64875 0

Will is taken to the barbers by his mother. While he is waiting, Will decides on a very unusual hairstyle! The barber cuts and combs and cuts and combs, until he gives Will exactly what he wants. Now Will really does look different for his school party. When he arrives everyone looks a little shocked and amazed, but then they all want a haircut too! Created in the 1990s by Olof and Lena Landström, the cartoon-style character of Will has become very popular in Sweden. This is a witty picture book that has a wonderful humorous visual style that children will love. Other titles in the series are *Will Goes to the Post Office*, *Will Goes to the Beach* and *Will's New Cap*.

Flop-Ear and his Friends
Guido van Genechten

Translated from Dutch
Cat's Whiskers (2004) HB £10.99 ISBN: 1 903012 71 6

Flop-Ear has lots of fun playing a variety of games with his friends in the forest. They play balance-the-carrot, fly-a-kite, leapfrog and trains. On a hill, hidden behind a tree, there stands a young, shy rabbit all by himself. He is different from the rest because the markings on his fur are not the same and he is not all one colour. When Flop-Ear sees him all by himself he invites him to join in the fun. This is a fantastic book for the very young about social inclusion, friendship and tolerance and it also conveys the poignant message that we all have something to learn from others. Flop-Ears is rapidly becoming an international best-selling literary character and there are another three books in the series: *Flop-Ear*, *Flop-Ear and Annie* and *Flop-Ear is Brave!*

The Best Bottom
Brigitte Minne, Illustrated by Marjolein Pottie

Translated from Dutch
Macmillan Children's Books (2003) PB £4.99 ISBN: 0 333 99287 3

Who has the best bottom of all? It is a question that none of the animals can answer! Is it Peacock, with his magnificent tail? or Rabbit with her soft, fluffy tail? or Pig, with his corkscrew tail? or even Frog, who has no tail at all? No one can agree so the animals decide to hold a best bottom competition. Everyone becomes fiercely competitive, but when the winner is finally announced, they are all in for a surprise! This is an amusing story by Brigitte Minnie accompanied by striking double-spread illustrations of the animals by Marjolein Pottie. This is a book that children will find fun and ideal for reading aloud.

The First Day at School
Yvonne Jagtenberg

Translated from Dutch
Cat's Whiskers (2002) PB £4.99 ISBN: 1 903012 56 2

It is the first day at school and Leo is very frightened of this unknown, new environment. He is reluctant to join in with the rest of the class in the various activities despite the other children trying to make him feel welcome. Eventually, Leo overcomes his anxieties by wearing a big grotesque wolf mask in a 'Little Red Riding Hood' play. This is a clever book where the wolf mask can also be perceived as a representation of a young boy's anxiety on his first day at school. The crayon, child-like, atmospheric illustrations are in perfect tune with this

poignant story of the fears of a child on the first day at school. This is a typical example of contemporary children's book illustration with a strong European flavour.

Ghost Party

Jacques Duquennoy

Translated from French by Antonia Parkin
Frances Lincoln (2004) HB £9.99 ISBN: 1 84507 325 8

Welcome to the ghost party and have plenty of fun following the hilarious events that happen during dinnertime in the great dining hall of the castle. Henry the ghost has decided to have a party and to invite six of his friends. While the guests sit comfortably at the dinner table, Henry flits back and forward to the kitchen bringing special drinks and dishes he has prepared. This is the typical picture book where readers need to look at the illustrations in order to follow the story. For instance, Henry offers a variety of drinks to his guests which result in each ghost changing their appearance and camouflaging themselves according to the colour of the beverage they have: blue, pink, yellow, green and the orange colour that comes from the pumpkin soup. *Ghost Party* was originally published in France in 1994 and it took ten long years to come to the UK. Look out for Jacques Duquennoy's new book, *Loch Ness Ghosts*, also published by Frances Lincoln.

Splosh!

Philippe Corentin

Translated from French by Sarah Pakenham
Andersen Press (2002) PB £3.99 ISBN: 0 86264 589 1

A very hungry wolf spies what he thinks is a big, round cheese at the bottom of a well. When he bends down to reach it he loses his balance and topples into the water where he soon realises that the 'big round cheese' is merely the reflection of the moon. Finding himself trapped in the well, he tricks a passer-by into rescuing him. There is a neat twist at the end of this book as the sly wolf gets what he deserves in the end. Philippe Corentin is well known in France as an illustrator of humorous picture books. *Splosh!* is a highly original book with bright, comic illustrations that children will love.

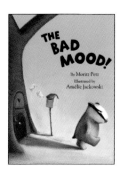

The Bad Mood!

Moritz Petz, illustrated by Amélie Jackowski

Translated from German by J. Alison James
North-South Books (2004) HB £9.99 ISBN: 0 7358 1888 6

"Humph" said Badger when he woke up one morning, "I'm in a bad mood today!" He decides that he had better stay at home, but at breakfast Badger reconsiders. After all, what is the point of being in a bad mood if nobody knows how miserable he feels? So Badger sets out, slamming the door behind him. He spreads his bad mood everywhere he goes, greeting all his friends with angry, rude remarks, which in turn, puts them all in a bad mood as well! By afternoon Badger has come up with a way to get rid of his bad mood, now all he has to do is cheer up the other animals too. This is a delightful picture book by Moritz Petz, with rich, expressive double-spread watercolour illustrations. An ideal book for young children that explains with humour the experience of being in a bad mood and its effects on others.

Pirate Pete Sets Sail

Jean-Pierre Jâggi, illustrated by Alan Clarke

Translated from German by J. Alison James
North-South Books (2003) HB £9.99 ISBN: 0 7358 1832 0

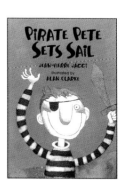

Pirate Pete and his mates are setting sail for a new island. It is hard work loading all their treasure onto the ship, but they manage to cast off and sail across the seas until they finally spot their new island. This is a lovely story about a boy who is concerned about moving to a new house with his parents. He decides to turn it into an exciting adventure – the house is the pirates' den, the car a ship and the motorway service station is a filthy harbour – and, of course, he is the pirate captain. This is an ideal book for parents to use if they are planning to move house. Very lively and vibrant illustrations by Alan Clarke, full of colour that will attract any young child.

Boris's Glasses

Peter Cohen, illustrated by Olof Landström

Translated from Swedish by Joan Sandin
R&S Books (2003) HB £8.99 ISBN: 91 29 65942 6

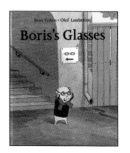

Boris's television picture is blurry but the TV repairman tells him that the problem is with his eyesight – not the TV! A trip to the opticians confirms the diagnosis – Boris needs glasses. When he gets his new glasses, he realises that he can now see everything clearly and he decides that he should get a job. He had no idea that there was so much to look at or that Gudrun in the bakery was so pretty! This is a delightful picture book by Peter Cohen, with comic illustrations by Olof Landström that are both vibrant and full of detail, particularly of Boris's home and where he works. There is no doubt that children will love this quirky tale.

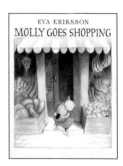

Molly Goes Shopping

Eva Eriksson

Translated from Swedish by
Elisabeth Kallick Dyssegaard
R&S Books (2003) HB £7.99
ISBN: 91 29 65819 5

A Crash Course for Molly

Eva Eriksson

Translated from Swedish by
Elisabeth Kallick Dyssegaard
R&S Books (2005) HB £7.99
ISBN: 91 29 66156 0

Molly is confident that she can now do things on her own, like going shopping. When Grandma sends her to the shop to buy beans, Molly is happy to go, but as she arrives at the busy shop she completely forgets what she is supposed to buy and comes back with potatoes instead! When Grandma asks Molly what

happened, she tells her that the shopkeeper insisted that she buy the potatoes. However, Molly gets caught out in her lie after Grandma goes to the shop to sort out the mystery.

In *A Crash Course for Molly*, Molly is learning to ride a bike and she loves it! The only problem is that she keeps running into things. She keeps her eye on the objects in her path – like poles and people – but for some reason, she still hits them. Luckily, she receives some good advice from the local driving instructor. Eva Eriksson has illustrated many children's books in Sweden and was the recipient of the *Astrid Lindgren Award* in 2001. These are delightful stories, accompanied by vivid, humorous illustrations, conveying a simple message that children can learn from and understand.

The Rabbit Who Didn't Want to Go to Sleep

Lilian Edvall, illustrated by Sara Gimbergsson

Translated from Swedish by Elisabeth Kallick Dyssegaard
R&S Books (2004) HB £8.99 ISBN: 91 29 66001 7

Rabbit is tired and he still wants to play with his toy cars. He's even made an extra-cool track to race them on. His mum tells him it's time for bed, but it can't be true! The rabbit plots and pleads to stay up longer, and at first Mum and Dad are willing to give him some more time. But then he manages to wake up his little sister! This charming story, accompanied by warm-hued illustrations by Sara Gimbergsson, captures every child's desire to stay up a little past their bedtime. Another book about Rabbit by Lilian Edvall is *The Rabbit Who Longed for Home*, also published by North-South Books.

In the Land of Elves

Daniela Drescher

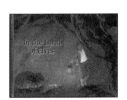

Translated from German
Floris Books (2005) HB £6.99 ISBN: 0 86315 484 0

As springtime arrives the elves leave their shelter to come outside and join their animal companions, working and collecting food as well as playing amongst the roots and trees. This short story, written in rhyming couplets, follows the lives of the elves through the different seasons, from spring, through summer, autumn and finally winter, when they return to the warmth of their shelter while they wait for the spring to return again. The charming, double page illustrations bring alive the secret world of the elves and will enchant any young reader.

Santa's Littlest Helper

Anu Stohner, illustrated by Henrike Wilson

Translated from German by Anna Trenter
North-South Books (2004) HB £9.99 ISBN: 0 7475 7574 6

Santa's littlest Helper gets very excited about Christmas. He is always the first to wash his sleigh, polish his boots, wrap his beautiful handmade presents and bake

his cakes and gingerbread. But every year on Christmas Eve, Santa Claus tells the little Helper that he can't allow him to deliver the presents because he is just too small! Sadly he returns home prepared to have a lonely night by the fire. In the evening, when everything is quiet, the little Helper goes for a moon-light stroll in the forest where he makes an exciting discovery! This is a warm, touching story by Anu Stohner with a lovely message about the Christmas spirit. The artwork by Henrike Wilson is bold and striking and the characters are emphasised with a black outline contrasting with the vivid reds and whites on the double-page spread.

Felipa and the Day of the Dead
Birte Müller

Translated from German by Marianne Martens
North-South Books (2004) HB £9.99 ISBN: 0 7358 1894 0

When Felipa's beloved grandmother Abuelita dies she feels terribly sad. In an attempt to comfort Felipa, her parents tell her that when people die their souls live on forever and that Abuelita's soul is with the spirits, high up in the mountains. Felipa decides to try and find Abuelita's soul and she sets off towards the mountains. When her dad finds her, he explains that souls live in their own world, but every year in November they come to visit and there is a big celebration. The long awaited day of celebration arrives and Felipa feels close to Abuelita again. A wonderful picture book that introduces children to the feelings of loss and death in a very sensitive way. The simple, almost childlike illustrations bring to life the rich colours of traditional South American culture.

Hammer Soup
Ingrid and Dieter Schubert

Translated from Dutch
Andersen Press (2004) HB £10.99 ISBN: 1 84270 367 6

Kate keeps her house and garden very tidy and she never shares her vegetables with anyone. One morning she is rudely awakened by the sound of banging. A giant has moved in next door and is building a monstrosity of a house. Brian the giant tries to be friendly but Kate is having none of it and sets to work fencing in her garden. Throughout the summer while Kate works, Brian plays, ignoring all the repairs that should be done to his house. Soon he begins to realise that he should have taken Kate's advice, when his house is blown away in a raging storm. Kate invites the cold and hungry Brian into her house, although she is reluctant to give him any of her food. Brian provides the solution by suggesting that he makes some delicious hammer soup! Vivid caricature style of artwork by this husband and wife team, full of detail, makes this an ideal book to share with young children.

Max Velthuijs
Frog in Love

Frog in Love
Max Velthuijs
Translated from Dutch by Anthea Bell
Andersen Press (1999) PB £4.99
ISBN: 0 86264 872 6

Frog is Sad
Max Velthuijs
Translated from Dutch
Andersen Press (2005) PB £4.99
ISBN: 1 84270 427 3

Frog Finds a Friend
Max Velthuijs
Translated from Dutch
Andersen Press (2004) PB £4.99
ISBN: 1 84270 213 0

The Frog books by illustrator Max Velthuijs have become contemporary classics and the delightful amphibian in his stripy shorts has acquired an international reputation. Frog can be many things – vulnerable, thoughtful, impulsive, wise, compassionate, frightened – and these books follow the lives of Frog and his friends Duck, Pig, Rat and Hare.

Frog in Love was the first Frog book published in 1989. Frog is worried about his health because his heart beats too fast and he is walking about as if in a dream, he goes hot and cold and he feels like laughing and then crying. Hare tells him he must be in love – but who is he in love with?

Frog is Sad
Max Velthuijs

In *Frog Finds a Friend*, Frog discovers a little bear that is lost and decides to take him home to be his new friend. Frog looks after the little bear and teaches him everything that he knows to the other animals' great surprise. They do everything together and they are the best of friends. Then one day Little Bear decides he must go away, back to where he came from. Frog is heartbroken and wonders whether he will ever see Little Bear again.

In *Frog is Sad*, Frog is overcome by sadness but he doesn't know why. He doesn't feel like smiling, in fact he feels like crying and wants to be left alone. Rat tries to cheer him up by playing him some music on his violin but he only succeeds in making Frog cry! But at last, Frog starts to laugh and soon he has all his friends laughing with him.

Other issues are tackled with the gentle humour so characteristic of these stories. The subject of death appears in *Frog and the Birdsong*; accepting difference and dealing with the prejudice shown by the other animals in *Frog and the Stranger*, getting lost in *Frog in Winter* and exploring the wider world in *Frog and the Wide World*. Max Velthuijs's perceptive and beautiful illustrations make these books popular with young children and are ideal for reading aloud. Other titles are: *Frog and the Treasure*, *Frog is Frog*, *Frog is a Hero*, *Frog and a Very Special Day*. Four of the Frog titles are also available in dual-language (see page 92).

Frog
Finds a Friend
Max Velthuijs

'If we wish to cross borders, we must also cross language barriers' Lene Kaaberbo

The Surprise

Sylvia van Ommen

Translated from Dutch
WingedChariot Press (2005) HB £8.99 ISBN: 1 90534 103 2

Have you ever been lucky enough to see a sheep weighing herself on scales or riding a Vespa? Prepare yourself to witness all this and much more in this hilarious picture book from the Netherlands and now published in the UK for the delight of young readers. Sheep does not wait for anyone to trim her wool. She has already made up her mind and starts to trim her woolly body herself. Then she goes to the shop and buys some coloured dye, gets on her motorbike, sorts a few things out and finally surprises a very good friend! This is one of four European picture books being published this year by WingedChariot Press. *The Surprise* is a wordless picture book – you do not need words to savour it though – it is not a translation in the true sense of the word, but it has been included in *Outside In* to show that visual narrative can successfully cross international borders. *The Surprise* is Sylvia Van Ommen's second book and shows her diversity of unique styles at work.

Ed Loves Sarah Loves Tim

Edith Schreiber-Wicke, illustrated by Carola Holland

Cat's Whiskers (2000) HB £10.99 ISBN: 1 90301 214 7

Ed experiences a very special feeling every time Sarah looks at him, and when she asks him to be her boyfriend everything seems wonderful. But one day Ed arrives late at school and finds Sarah busy talking to Tim, and later he discovers her holding Tim's hand. Ed feels rejected and lonely. But after a few days, everything changes and he feels that same special feeling again, because he has made a new friend. A charming story that follows the emotions through different stages of friendship – from rejection and misery to finding a new friend. The soft pastel illustrations complement this gentle story, making it an ideal picture book for parents and teachers to share with children.

Yours and Mine

Peter Geibler, illustrated by Almud Kunert

Translated from German by Anthea Bell
Frances Lincoln (2005) HB £10.99 ISBN: 1 84507 323 1

Two friends, a girl and a boy, embark on a fantastic trip as they compare their imaginary friends in a poem that has been adapted into a picture book. The striking qualities lie in the stunning surreal illustrations that perfectly match the spirit of the text. The small figures of the boy and the girl are lost in their enormous and disproportionate surroundings. The story offers lots of potential for imaginative discussion between parent/carer and child. There is a complete version of the poem on one page at the end of the book. A thoroughly innovative picture book from Germany full of amazing artistic qualities and revealing different styles and techniques.

The Moon Has Written You a Poem: Poems to Read to Children on Moonlit Nights

José Jorge Letria, illustrated by André Letria

Translated from Portuguese by Maurice Riordan
WingedChariot Press (2005) HB £12.99 ISBN: 1 905341 00 8

This picture book from Portugal is a good example of how much the children's book publishing market has progressed and developed there over the last few years. It is an ideal book to read aloud and also for bedtime reading, as the poetic language is highly evocative and touching with a melodic flavour that perfectly suits its purpose. Any young child will fall asleep peaceful and serene after listening to the rhythmical sound of the words, travelling in their imagination to the fantastic places mentioned in the story: poems full of dreams, words with beautiful sounds, light and magic, all this is to be found here. The surreal illustrations by André Letria are touching and full of mystery and constitute the predominant part of the double-page spread.

Finn Cooks

Birte Müller

Translated from German by J. Alison James
North-South Books (2004) HB £9.99 ISBN: 0 7358 1935 1

Like most children Finn does not like healthy, balanced meals and when his mother explains to him that the body needs protein and calcium, he is not convinced by her recommendations. Finn would much rather have something more exciting instead like chocolate or sweets. One evening Finn proposes exchanging duties with his parents for just one day and to be in charge of the shopping and the kitchen. When he goes to the supermarket he gets carried away and comes back home with all his favourite foods. Finn suffers the consequences though, when his recipe of chocolate doughnuts and cheese curls has an adverse effect and he ends up with a terrible tummy ache. This is a picture book that will be useful for parents and carers who are trying to put forward to their children the idea of a sensible balanced diet. The message is put across brilliantly and without being didactic or educational and the bright, colourful illustrations are highly expressive and superbly match the spirit of the text.

Don't Look Under the Bed!

Angelika Glitz, illustrated by Imke Sönnichsen

Translated from German
Cat's Whiskers (2000) PB £4.99 ISBN: 1 90301 227 9

Every child is scared of that 'imaginary' monster that lives under the bed and Tom is no exception. Even though he endeavours to fall asleep, strange noises prevent him from doing so. When his mum comes to say good night, Tom shares his fears with her, but she has an explanation for everything! The vroooommmm noise is coming from the cars outside, while the rattle, rattle noise comes from the wind and as for the big shadows on the wall, there is also an explanation for that too. Despite his mum's attempts to reassure him, Tom remains unhappy and tells her that she has forgotten to look under the bed where she is in for a surprise! This funny story has filmic qualities with touches of action and suspense. The mum and son relationship is delightful and children will be amused by the incidents that take place and the double-spread illustration by Imke Sönnichsen brings this story alive.

Laura's Secret

Klaus Baumgart

Translated from German by Judy Waite
Little Tiger Press (2003) PB £5.99 ISBN: 85430 981 1

One rainy evening Laura and her little brother Tommy make a home-made kite that they can't wait to take to the park to try out. When some horrible boys ruin their kite so that it can no longer fly, Laura turns to her special friend 'the star' and pleads for some help. Tom and Laura want a special kind of kite that can fly as high as the stars. This is a magical book with illustrations by Klaus Baumgart that touches in a sensitive way on the problem of bullying of younger children. The Laura's Star series is an international best-seller and there are several titles in the series, *Laura's Star*, *Laura's Christmas Star*, *Laura's Star and the Sleepover* and a *Laura's Star* Sticker Activity Book.

Those Messy Hempels

Brigitte Luciani, illustrated by Vanessa Hié

Translated from German by J. Alison James
North-South Books (2004) HB £9.99 ISBN: 0 7358 1909 2

The Hempels are a messy family. Nothing is ever in the right place, there is clutter everywhere and they live in permanent chaos. But they don't normally mind until they decide to bake a cake and can't find the whisk! This makes them realise that it's time to clean up and get things organised. As they tidy up and hunt for the whisk it leads them on a hilarious cleaning spree as they find other objects that belong in different parts of the house, but in the end they succeed in finding the missing utensil. *Those Messy Hempels* is a zany story that children will love. It is ideal for reading aloud as it has lots of repetition and interaction. For instance such questions are asked as; 'where does the pillow belong, in the kitchen?' or 'where does the toothbrush belong, in the bedroom?' A perfect book for parents and carers to use when trying to get children to tidy up! The impressive artwork is highly amusing and the geometrical, cardboard-like shape of the characters has a certain theatrical appeal that makes it child-friendly and very enjoyable.

Pirate Girl

Cornelia Funke,
illustrated by Kerstin Meyer

Translated from German by Chantal Wright
The Chicken House (2005) HB £10.99
ISBN: 1 904442 49 8

The Princess Knight

Cornelia Funke,
illustrated by Kerstin Meyer

Translated from German by Anthea Bell
The Chicken House (2003) PB £5.99
ISBN: 1 904442 14 5

Here are two picture books about feisty young heroines by international author, Cornelia Funke. In *Pirate Girl* Molly has been kidnapped for a ransom by the ferocious Captain Firebeard and his crew aboard the Horrible Haddock, that rules the high seas. Molly is made to peel potatoes, clean boots, patch sails and scrub decks, but despite all this she won't reveal who she is. Soon she proves to be sharper and quicker than any of the pirate gang and skilfully manages to outwit them. Before long, Firebeard must face the fury of Barbarous Bertha, Molly's mother!

In *The Princess Knight* Princess Violetta wants to be as strong and brave as her three brothers are, despite her size. They are taught riding, jousting and fighting with swords and the King decides that his daughter will be taught exactly the same lessons. Constantly being teased and laughed at by her siblings as she struggles to acquire the same skills, Violetta is determined that she will succeed. At night she slips out into the woods and secretly teaches herself. As she becomes nimble and quick even her brothers stop making fun of her and calling her 'Itsy-Bitsy Little Vi'. Soon she is ready for the greatest battle of all – the tournament that will decide her future. Cornelia Funke has produced a delightful picture book full of humour that children will enjoy. The engaging text is accompanied by Kerstin Meyer's bright and bold cartoon-like illustrations that took their inspiration from the Bayeux Tapestry.

Good Night, Alfie Atkins

Gunilla Bergström

Translated from Swedish by Elisabeth Kallick Dyssegaard
R&S Books (2005) HB £7.99 ISBN: 91 29 66154 4

Alfie Atkins, like a lot of four-year-olds, sometimes doesn't want to go to bed. There will always be many reasons why he cannot go to sleep and he certainly manages to think up quite a few! Luckily for him, he has a very patient dad, but even he can become exhausted. Alfie Atkins is one of the most loved picture book characters in Sweden and has become a classic in Scandinavian children's literature. There are more than 30 titles in this series that have become an international success. The particular charm of Gunilla Bergström's work is her highly imaginative illustrations.

My Very Own Lighthouse

Francisco Cunha

Translated from Portuguese by Joäo Leal
WingedChariot Press (2005) HB £10.99 ISBN: 1 905341 01 6

A young girl lives in a small fishing village where her father is a fisherman. At bedtime she has horrible nightmares about her dad navigating the dangerous waters during the stormy nights. She goes to her mum for comfort and is reassured that her dad is safe, because wherever he is, a lighthouse will always look after him. Then she has a wonderful idea – she'll build her very own 'lighthouse of love' with the help of her toys – to help guide her dad on his final return home. This is a touching picture book of hope, which highlights the fears of a young child, drawing on the experience of a small district in Portugal, where the men leave their families behind to work at sea. A debut picture book for Francisco Cunha, it has a universal value and poetic message about the absence of the paternal figure. The dramatic pictures are in perfect harmony with the spirit of the text.

Bertil and the Bathroom Elephants

Inger Lindahl and Eva Lindström

Translated from Swedish by Elisabeth Kallick Dyssegaard
R&S Books (2003) HB £8.99 ISBN: 91 29 65944 2

Bertil likes to splash a lot of water when he has a bath and he thinks it's fun when two mischievous elephants join him. Their trunks can really spray the water everywhere! After a while though, it gets too much even for Bertil and he longs to have peace in the bathroom. It's not Bertil's fault that the bathroom gets so wet but how do you get rid of naughty bathroom elephants? Eventually a solution is found and Bertil can sit in peace and quiet in his bathroom. This is a delightful story by Inger Lindahl accompanied by charming, funny water-colour illustrations that will appeal to any child that gets carried away while having a bath.

The Dance of the Eagle and the Fish

Aziz Nesin, illustrated by Kağan Güner

Adapted by Alison Boyle Translated from Turkish by Ruth Christie
Milet Publishing (2001) PB £4.99 ISBN: 1 84059 316 4

From the highest peak, Kartal the ancient eagle contemplates the whole world beneath. He feels powerful and strong and is reassured in the knowledge that his figure is embodied in flags and shields all over the world. But while Kartal is fearless overland, he remains scared and powerless in front of the enormity of the sea. Then Balik, the fish queen of the seas, leaps from its depths and meets Kartal. They both become attracted to each other and rapidly fall in love. But how can their love survive while one needs the sky and the other the sea? The poetic narrative beautifully complements the sentimental nature of this traditional Turkish tale, while the colourful watercolour illustrations by Kağan Güner represent a style that has not been previously seen in picture books for children in this country and which will bring pure joy to the eye.

Little Polar Bear and the Husky Pup

Hans de Beer

Translated from German by Rosemary Lanning
North-South Books (2004) PB £4.99 ISBN: 0 7358 1904 1

Lars the little Polar Bear is one of the many creations by well-known author and illustrator, Hans de Beer. Lars lives at the North Pole and during one of his excursions he walks further than usual and discovers Flo, a husky pup who is stuck in a deep crack in the ice. Despite his fear of huskies, Lars rescues him and decided to help him find the rest of the husky team – a task full of danger and surprises! The illustrations are soft and capture the often bleak landscape of the polar region. This series of polar bear books are available in dual-language (see page 92). Other titles by Hans de Beer available from North-South Books are *Leonardo's Dream* about a small penguin who dreams of learning to fly and *Oh No, Ono!* about a boisterous piglet's enthusiastic exploration of a farm.

Mole's Journey

E.T.W. Igel, illustrated by Jakob Kirchmayr

Translated from German by Sibylle Kazeroid
North-South Books (2004) HB £9.99 ISBN: 0 7358 1879 7

One day Mole catches a cold and has to take to his bed. He feels terrible, one minute he is shivering and sneezing and the next he is burning with fever. As Mole snuggles down into his bed he thinks about his dream of travelling the world. Strangely enough, Mole's cold symptoms are reflected in his journey as he begins to dig through underground tunnels – to the freezing North Pole, the sweltering heat of the desert, the tallest mountains where the air is so dry and finally to the deep jungle that is steamy and humid. When Mole gets back from his world tour he finds his friends sitting by his bed. His cold is cured and he has discovered that there is no place like home. A wonderful book for all those who are not well but don't want to get bored lying in bed. This is a heart-warming story with beautiful, vibrant illustrations by Sibylle Kirchmayr. An ideal picture book to read aloud or for independent reading.

Roberta and Me
Sibylle and Jürgen Rieckhoff

Translated from the German by Vera Müller
Frances Lincoln (2004) HB £10.99 ISBN: 184507 324 X

For a girl from the city it is love at first sight when she meets Roberta for the first time. Roberta the sheep seems like the perfect pet because she is clever, clean and sociable. But city life isn't easy for Roberta – there is the lift to be negotiated, eating meals at the table with the family and trips to the supermarket – and even though she adapts well to the new rules, the family soon begin to wonder if Roberta might be pining for something more. This is a charming story inspired by a seaside holiday that the authors took with their daughter, Johanna. She also met her perfect sheep – although her wish to take him home only came true in book form! Amusing, cartoon-like illustrations make this a fun book that children will identify with.

Milo and the Mysterious Island
Marcus Pfister

Translated from German by Marianne Martens
North-South Books (2000) HB £12.99 ISBN: 0 7358 1352 3

Part of the Milo series, this book is the sequel to *Milo and the Magical Stones*. Milo the cliff mouse is bored and restless and he longs to go off exploring to see what lies over the horizon. Milo tells the other mice about his dream and of his idea of making a giant raft so that they can sail across the sea. This reminds wise old Balthazar of the ancient tale about a mysterious island inhabited by striped mice. They all join forces to build a raft and – with their glittering magical stones to light their way – set sail in search of the island. There is a clever alternative-ending format halfway through the story whereby the book splits into two sections, allowing young children to participate in the story and decide whether it will have a happy or sad ending. This is a large format book with the use of simple shapes and soft outlines that are characteristic of Marcus Pfister's work.

Super H
Olivier Douzou and Philippe Derrien
Translated by Sarah Adams
Milet Publishing (2002) HB £7.99 ISBN: 1 84059 333 4

When Henry receives a mysterious parcel addressed to 'Mr Henry', he finds it contains a superhero outfit. He hasn't heard of 'Super H' – not on TV, or at the movies, or in newspapers! However, he soon realises that his costume has great potential and he names himself 'Super H' speculating about the 'important' duties of a superhero. He can learn how to behave better and to be brave as well as lots of other things. His mother doesn't share his enthusiasm and drags him off to the supermarket – where he gets a nasty surprise! This is an unusual, funny and original picture book from France. The illustrations and design have been carefully thought out and there are lots of intricate details to ensure readers will revisit the story again and again.

The Day Adam Got Mad
Astrid Lindgren, Illustrated by Marit Törnqvist
Translated from Swedish by Barbara Lucas
R&S Books (1993) HB £7.95 ISBN: 91 29 62064 3

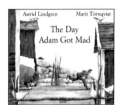

From Sweden comes this hilarious tale of a huge good-natured bull called Adam who lives in a quiet, sleepy country town in a barn with lots of cows and calves. On a bright sunny Easter Sunday, Adam breaks loose; he is in a dangerous mood and comes thundering down the hill. Everyone in the town is terrified, but seven-year-old Karl, a young farm boy who talks to animals, has a plan that will surprise everyone! The story of this very young Swedish bullfighter is one of the many books by the international, award-winning author of the classic *Pippi Longstocking*. Marit Törnqvist's watercolour illustrations magnificently interpret the humorous text and have filmic attributes that give the right pace to the story. Perfect for storytime, bedtime reading or reading aloud.

Lotta's Easter Surprise
Astrid Lindgren, illustrated by Ilon Wikland
Translated from Swedish by Patricia Crampton
R&S Books (1991) HB £7.95 ISBN: 91 29 62018 X

What sort of Easter will it be without chocolate-covered Easter eggs? Every year without fail, families await the arrival of the Easter Bunny to deliver the eggs before Easter Sunday. But when Lotta discovers that the only sweet shop in the village has closed down and that the owner is going back to Greece, she wonders how they are going to get their Easter treats. However, the sweet shop owner provides a solution and Lotta ends up with her own secret supply to save the day. Astrid Lindgren is Sweden's most widely read author and this is one of the many books she wrote about Lotta. The amazing illustrations by Ilon Wikland complement this gentle story.

Andrei's Search
Barbro Lindgren, illustrated by Eva Eriksson
Translated from Swedish by Elisabeth Kallick Dyssegaard
R&S Books (2000) HB £8.99 ISBN: 91 29 64756 8

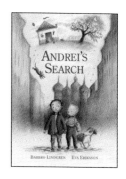

Andrei and his friend, Vova live in a children's home. Andrei had a mother, but she has disappeared and Vova never knew his. They wander around the city of St Petersburg searching for Andrei's mother. She has been gone for so long now that he can barely remember what her eyes looked like. They watch the trams, eat pierogis – dumplings filled with vegetables, fruit or cheese – and adopt a friendly dog as they continue their search. At long last, their persistence seems finally to be rewarded. Barbro Lindgren explores a child's imagination in this tale of longing and dreaming, that is accompanied by soft, watercolour illustrations by Eva Eriksson.

Julia Wants a Pet
Barbro Lindgren and Eva Eriksson
Translated from Swedish by Elisabeth Kallick Dyssegaard
R&S Books (2003) HB £8.99 ISBN: 91 29 65940 X

Each day Julia goes out to play pushing her baby carriage. She is on the look out for something to play with – ideally, a pet she can put in her carriage. Julia has always wanted a pet and most of all, she would like a pony, but a hedgehog or a frog would be fine, too. But today there are not many animals around – only crows that are too fast or flies that are too small. Then one day she spots a small boy and she wonders whether she can squeeze him into her baby carriage! A gentle, funny story by Barbro Lindgren with lovely, soft illustrations by Eva Eriksson that help convey this story of the longing of a young child for a pet of her own.

The Grandma Hunt
Nina Matthis, illustrated by Gunilla Kvarnström
Translated from Swedish by Elisabeth Kallick Dyssegaard
R&S Books (2002) HB £7.99 ISBN: 91 29 65656 7

Every summer Jacob goes to spend a week with his grandfather who lives in the country. Usually, they have a great time together, but this year his cousin Linnea joins them as well. At first Jacob is upset because she seems to be getting all of Grandpa's attention. But soon he and Linnea become friends and decide to give Grandpa the perfect birthday present. He is going to be 96 or 69, they don't know which, and they want to find him a new grandma! Bright, humorous illustrations by Gunilla Kvarnström accompany this lovely story by Nina Matthis of jealousy, friendship and concern for the loneliness that old age can bring.

Goldie at the Orphanage
Martha Sandwall-Bergström,
illustrated by Eva Stålsjö

Translated from Swedish
Floris Books (2004) HB £8.99
ISBN: 0 86315 443 3

Goldie at the Farm
Martha Sandwall-Bergström,
illustrated by Eva Stålsjö

Translated from Swedish
Floris Books (2005) HB £8.99
ISBN: 0 86315 485 9

Goldie is discovered as a baby by a fisherman after a shipwreck and is placed in an orphanage. She is lonely at first, but once a new girl, Lotta arrives, they soon become good friends and begin to have some fun. However, this comes to an abrupt end once they have turned seven years old. When children reach this age they must begin to work and every year there is an auction of orphans. The two girls will be auctioned off to the highest bidder and will have to adjust to a new life. In the sequel, *Goldie at the Farm*, Goldie is bought by a farmer to be a maid to his family. Although the family treats her well there are lots of chores and she longs to go to school like the other children. Martha Sandwall-Bergström based this story on her own experiences of growing up as a young girl in a poor area of Sweden. Eva Stålsjö's beautiful, lively watercolour illustrations complement this heart-warming story.

Sweets
Sylvia van Ommen

Translated from Dutch by Sylvia van Ommen and Neal Hoskins
WingedChariot Press (2005) HB £7.99 ISBN: 1 905341 02 4

Two friends text each other arranging to meet up in the park. Jori brings the sweets while Oscar is responsible for the drinks. Underneath the shadow of a big tree they eat their sweets and drink their coffee. But soon, inspired by the blue sky, they start to speculate about life after death. Would they be going up there? And, if so, would it be easy for them to meet? Would they encounter anyone else in heaven or would it be very crowded and impossible to recognise each other? Would there be sweets there? They start making sensible and practical arrangements and provisions for their future meeting. A picture book that tackles questions that most children tend to ask, but adults find difficult to answer. This is a wonderful, touching and very unusual picture book about friendship, illustrated in black-and-white line drawings that beautifully portray the deep philosophical message of the written text.

Grandpa's Angel
Jutta Bauer

Translated from German
Walker Books (2005) HB £9.99 ISBN: 1 84428 034 9

'Nothing could ever hurt me' Grandpa explains to his grandson when he goes to visit him in hospital. He tells his grandson about his life and how every morning as a boy, he would run past the big statue of an angel on his way to school,

and no matter what happened, nothing could touch him – he was nearly run over by a bus, almost fell down a hole, was chased by scary geese and did many daring things – but he was never afraid. Even through the dangerous times when the Nazis were in power and during the war that followed, through hunger and unemployment in its aftermath and all the strange things that life threw at him, Grandpa's angel was always nearby looking out for him. The angel is never specifically mentioned in the text but the illustrations show that it is never far from Grandpa's side. Always depicted in pale blue, invisible to everyone else – but whether Grandpa can see it we are not quite sure! This is a beautiful story, accompanied by gentle watercolour grey-green and ochre illustrations that make this a poignant and at times humorous picture book.

Abel and the Wolf
Sergio Lairla, illustrated by Alessandra Roberti

Translated from German by Marianne Martens
North-South Books (2004) HB £9.99 ISBN: 0 7358 1902 5

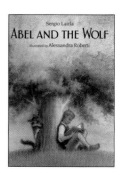

Now that Abel is old enough he needs to make his own way in the world. Together with the parting gifts from his parents – a walking stick, a knife, a large pot, some herbs and seeds, and a book with golden letters – Abel sets out on his journey. After travelling for many days, he finds a clearing in the forest and settles down to build himself a house and plant a garden. However, he is not alone, for the forest belongs to a wolf. Wolf is very suspicious and becomes angry and jealous as he watches Abel's every move. He deviously plots to attack Abel and steal everything he owns but his attempts fail miserably. In time, mistrust turns into friendship as Abel uses the gifts from his parents to find ways to turn a fearsome foe into a faithful friend. A wonderful, poetic story by Sergio Lairla, accompanied by bold, strong illustrations by Alessandra Roberti.

The Little Jester
Helena Olofsson

Translated from Swedish by Kjersti Board
R&S Books (2002) HB £8.99 ISBN: 91 29 65499 8

One evening, a boy jester arrives at a French monastery where he seeks food and shelter. After he has been well fed, he decides to thank the Monks by giving them a performance. He begins to juggle and dance and soon has them all laughing heartily. Investigating the noise, the Abbot is about to throw the jester out for disrespectful behaviour. But the monks notice that something wonderful has happened to their picture of the Madonna, and it is nothing less than a miracle! A vibrant picture book by Helena Olofsson with stunning watercolour illustrations blending medieval and modern pictorial language in this warm-hearted story about the power of laughter.

Abby
Wolfram Hänel, illustrated by Alan Marks

Translated from German by Rosemary Lanning
North-South Books (1996) HB £7.99 ISBN: 1 55858 648 2

This story is set on a very small island off the Irish coast, inhabited by just a few people. Abby is a dog owned by Moira, a young girl who is not very good at maths, especially as she spends most of the time daydreaming about her dog who is her best friend. Moira and Abbey enjoy life together running and playing freely in the meadows and on the beaches. However, their happiness is soon interrupted when Abby accidentally eats some poisonous meat. The prognosis for Abbey looks grim but Moira refuses to give up hope and spends long hours nursing Abby and coaxing her back to life. Wolfram Hänel based *Abby* on a true story from a small village in Kilnarovanagh in southern Ireland. Rosemary Lanning's translation from the original German reads with fluency and at the right pace. This is a moving story for children who are just beginning to develop their reading skills and is part of the 'Easy Read' series.

Spiny
Jürgen Lassig, illustrated by Uli Waas

Translated from German by J. Alison James
North-South Books (1995) PB £4.50 ISBN: 1 55858 552 4

This story is set sixty-five million years ago in the times of the dinosaurs. A small egg suddenly cracks and a tiny spinosaurus comes out of it, but there are still three other eggs to hatch. His is named Spiny and he is hungry and curious about his surroundings. Father and Mother Spinosaurus go out in search of food and leave him in the care of Igu, a friendly iguanodon dinosaur. However, soon Spiny gets lost and is caught by the dangerous TyRoar who does not have his best interests at heart! Luckily, harmony is restored when the courageous Igu rescues the tiny spinosaurus from TyRoar's big claws. This is the ideal 'Easy to Read' story for all those dinosaur fans and particularly boys.

The Other Side of the Bridge
Wolfram Hänel, illustrated by Alex de Wolf

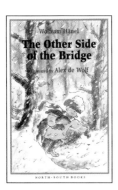

Translated from German by J. Alison James
North-South Books (1996) PB £4.50 ISBN: 1 55858 203 9

Andy is not the sort of boy who likes sports and he would rather spend his free time studying nature. Because Andy is quite short and doesn't join the other boys in their activities, he is repeatedly bullied. There are rumours that on the other side of the bridge there lives an old grumpy man called Jasper and he eats children! Driven by curiosity Andy decides to investigate, but on the way he gets trapped in a snowstorm. The next thing he knows is that he wakes up to find himself in the house of old Jasper who has saved his life. When Andy returns home he is able to reveal the truth about the old man and to dispel all the prejudice that has been built up around him. Another book in the 'Easy Read' series.

King Bobble

Marianne Busser and Ron Schröder,
illustrated by Hans de Beer

Translated from German by J. Alison James
North-South Books (1996) PB £4.50 ISBN: 1 55858 202 0

Plump, fun-loving and not too bright, King Bobble and his queen cavort through life wearing wheels instead of crowns. Their solutions to life's little problems (from dirty feet to a runny nose) are always different, and somehow they manage to find time for fun and games, like when they go missing and the police find them hanging from the coat rack hidden behind all the coats. Newly independent readers will be hugely entertained by the Bobbles' bizarre logic and bubbling high spirits. Full of humour and nonsense, another of the 'Easy to Read' books which children will treasure for years to come.

The Upside-Down Reader

Wilhelm Gruber, illustrated by Marlies Rieper-Bastian

Translated from German by J. Alison James
North-South Books (1998) PB £4.50 ISBN: 1 55858 307 8

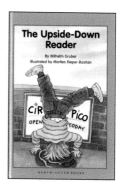

Tina has just started school and is very possessive about her books and back-pack. Her younger brother Tim still needs to wait a year before going to school, although he is eager to learn to read despite his sister's reluctance to teach him. Dad suggests that Tim can sit opposite his sister at the table while she is doing her homework. This way, and without anyone's knowledge, Tim learns to read upside down and then surprises everyone when they discover his precocious talent. When grandma comes to visit she takes the responsibility of teaching Tim to read properly. This is an amusing 'Easy to Read' story ideal for children who are just starting to develop an interest in reading. The bright colourful illustrations on each page make the story easy to understand as well as creating a pleasurable reading experience for any young child.

The Princess Gift Book

Tiny Fissher, illustrated by Barbara de Wolf

Translated from Dutch by Sally Miedema
Bloomsbury Children's Books (2001) HB £10.99 ISBN: 0 7475 55110 3

Four different stories about princesses are contained in this fun activity book about how to be a princess. Princess Hoppity-Hup lives in the desert with her selfish father, the Sultan, who won't let anyone use his sand! Princess Rosalie is a traditional princess who believes herself to be ugly because her wicked stepmother has cast a spell on her. Princess Sparkle invites everyone to her party only to be nearly thwarted by a wicked witch and Princess Oceana's wish to visit the sea is fulfilled in a very unusual way! At the beginning of each story practical tips are provided on how to dress like each princess using old clothes, strips of material, ribbon etc. Ideas range from making a princess handbag out of a marble bag and filling it with either beads, buttons, dried beans or uncooked macaroni – these ingredients also come in useful for Princess Oceana's noisy skirt! – to white plastic beakers for sleeves, a cushion for a skirt bustle, cotton wool balls to make a necklace and decorations made with potato cut-outs and paint on the material. Ideal for all those princess-mad girls!

Hen-sparrow Turns Purple

Gita Wolf, illustrated by Pulak Biswas

Tara Publications (2002) HB £14.99 ISBN: 81 86211 19 5

Hen-sparrow falls into a vat of dye and turns completely purple! This terrible calamity provokes a chain reaction of mourning throughout the land. This retelling of an old Indian tale has been exquisitely produced with silk-screen illustrations on brown paper and hand-pasted coloured artwork on every page. The illustrations are reminiscent of elaborate Indian miniature paintings. Designed in a very original accordion-style, this book can be used as a wall-hanging, making it ideal for teachers or storytellers to read aloud. *Hen-sparrow Turns Purple* won the *Biennale of Illustrations*, Bratislava, in 1999.

Hallo? Is Anybody There?

Jostein Gaarder, illustrated by Sally Gardner

Translated from Norwegian by James Anderson
Orion Children's Books (1998) PB £4.99 ISBN: 1 85881 623 8

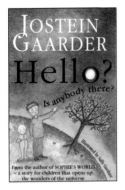

In the hours before his brother is born, eight-year-old Joe discovers an unusual visitor in his garden. Mika is from Eljo – where children hatch out of eggs and life in general is quite different from what Joe knows – and has fallen out of a spaceship, landing upside down in an apple tree. Mika and Joe become instant friends and spend the day discussing everything from dinosaurs and gravity to the origins of life on Earth and the wonders of the universe. Thought-provoking questions are framed within the illustrations such as "What would you say if you had a visit from outer space?" or "Can animals think?" The next morning Mika is gone, but Joe has a new-found appreciation for the wonders of the universe and a baby brother! The parallel between Mika and the new baby being born is a consistent theme throughout the story and it challenges young readers to look at the world afresh. Tender and enchanting, this book confirms Jostein Gaarder as an exceptional writer for children and Sally Gardner's whimsical line drawings complement the delightful story perfectly. Ideal for reading aloud to children or for independent reading.

The Wizard, the Ugly, and the Book of Shame
Pablo Bernasconi

Translated from Spanish (Argentina)
Bloomsbury Children's Books (2005) HR £10.99 ISBN: 0 7475 8123 1

Leitmeritz is a wizard – with a carrot nose – who lives in a castle at the top of a high hill. He is the sole proprietor of the powerful Book of Spells that has been passed down from generation to generation. It contains all the mysteries and secrets of the entire world and with the help of this book Leitmeritz is able to fulfil everyone's wishes, except that of his assistant, Chancery, who due to his physical appearance is named 'The Ugly'. While the master is away Chancery succumbs to temptation and decides to attempt to use the book and find a spell that will make him handsome. Unfortunately things go terribly wrong and on his return Leitmeritz notices that the spells in the book no longer work and disaster is unavoidable. This is a humorous, fantasy story that has all the elements of a modern classic and is wonderfully narrated. The collage-type illustrations are original in style and superb in every respect. Pablo Bernasconi's illustrated artwork is also featured on the front cover of this publication.

The Little Vampire
Angela Sommer-Bodenburg, illustrated by Amelie Glienke

Translated from German by Sarah Gibson
Andersen Press (2005) PB £4.99 ISBN: 1 84270 444 3

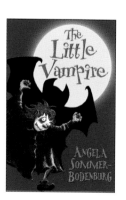

Andersen has brought out a brand new paperback edition – first translated into English in 1982 – of this well-known popular children's title. Nine-year-old Tony is a horror story addict – he reads anything from Frankenstein to Dracula and vampire tales – so he is rather alarmed when a little vampire called Rudolph lands on his windowsill one evening. This is the start of some hilarious adventures into the vampire world involving visits to Rudolph's home – The Vampire Family Vault – and having a close encounter with the cemetery keeper who is the vampires' sworn enemy. Tony hates the fact that his parents are so inquisitive about his new friends and in a moment of rashness, invites Rudolph and his sister, Anna, to tea to meet them! The Little Vampire is the first in the series and although written over 25 years ago (1979), it is still as popular as ever. There are a total of 18 'Little Vampire' books, which have been made into film and television series.

Bambert's Book of Missing Stories

Reinhardt Jung

Translated from German by Anthea Bell
Egmont Children's Books (2002) PB £4.99 ISBN: 0 7497 4705 6

In a small Austrian town, Bambert lives alone in an attic above his tenant Mr. Bloom's grocery shop. Because he is disabled, Bambert has difficulty in getting out into the world, but by night he sits at his window and dreams up stories which he writes into his Book of Wishes. Bambert has completed ten stories for his book and one day decides the stories should go and seek their own settings. Parcelling up each one, and sending it out into the world attached to a Japanese hot-air balloon, Bambert also includes an eleventh story, consisting only of four blank sheets of paper, for the recipient to invent. This book is something quite exceptional. It appears at first to be a set of fairy tales, yet each story has a pertinence to the life of its author, and all are set within the encompassing relationship between Bambert and Bloom. This produces a magical book of many layers, which would delight listeners from eight to eighty plus, and provide endless opportunities for classroom use.

The Boy Who Ate Stars

Kochka

Translated from French by Sarah Adams
Egmont Children's Books (2004) PB £4.99 ISBN: 1 4052 1129 6

When 12-year-old Lucy meets four-year-old Matthew, she encounters autism for the first time, and realizes not only how it isolates him from others, but also the insights and abilities he can access which remain dormant within 'normal' children. Contrary to the opinions of Lucy's parents and their establishment friends, the adults immediately concerned with Matthew think it best to allow him to develop in his own way and are caring but non-judgemental. Lucy and her North African friend Theo, together with Theo's grandfather, are similarly unbiased, and celebrate his individuality, and it is implied that the North African cultural background encourages a far more accepting attitude to 'difference'. Paralleled with Matthew's experience is that of François, the pampered pooch left in the care of Lucy's family, who is also permitted to follow his own destiny and escape the constraints of establishment expectations. This title retains the French atmosphere of the original, although it is questionable how transferable to young English readers is the experience of life in a Parisian apartment.

'*Vive la difference!* indeed, but how typical it is that this resounding phrase still as yet has no British equivalent!'

Nicholas Tucker

'From my perspective, it ain't what you lose but *how you gain it* in translation' Sarah Adams

The Christmas Mystery
Jostein Gaarder, illustrated by Sarah Gibb
Translated from Norwegian by Elizabeth Rokkan
Orion Children's Books (2003) PB £6.99 ISBN: 1 84255 282 1

While Christmas shopping with his dad Joachim finds a very old Advent Calendar that has been left in a bookshop by a mysterious flower-seller. When Joachim gets home, he realises that behind each of the twenty-four tiny doors, small pieces of paper have been hidden. Slowly, Joachim begins to uncover the story of a young girl, Elisabet Hansen, who disappeared from her home fifty years earlier and who travelled back through time across Europe to Palestine to find the Holy Family in Bethlehem. This book brings a contemporary twist to the traditional Christmas tale with its narration of two parallel stories – set fifty years apart. It is through Joachim and the magic Advent calendar that the two stories are allowed to eventually meet. The author skilfully captures the essence and mystery of Christmas bringing a freshness and sense of wonder in this extraordinary story that will be popular with both children and adults. This is a new abridged version with appealing illustrations by Sarah Gibb.

The Frog Castle
Jostein Gaarder, illustrated by Philip Hopman
Translated from Norwegian by James Anderson
Dolphin (Orion Children's Books) (2000) PB £3.99 ISBN: 1 85881 827 3

Gregory Peggory is not sure how it all began, but one night he finds himself outside and alone in the frozen snow. Down by the Newt Pond he meets Umpin, a boggart who transports him from the cold winter's night to a hot summer's day. After devouring pancakes and strawberry jam, Gregory Peggory reluctantly agrees to kiss a frog that needs to be turned back into a prince. He is taken to the Frog Castle and here he has to learn to be brave as he encounters the Newts who guard the castle, the wicked lord chamberlain, the bold and scary queen and the kind old king whose heart has been stolen. This is a magical story of adventure where dreams and reality are all mixed up together and nothing is what it seems. Jostein Gaarder is a wonderful storyteller whose special gift is to open children's eyes to the great mysteries of life. As with all his stories, there is a subtext, this time the gentle exploration of a child learning to come to terms with his grandfather's death.

Fattypuffs and Thinifers

André Maurois, illustrated by Fritz Wegner

Translated from French
Jane Nissen Books (2001) PB £4.99 ISBN: 1 903252 07 5

From France comes this hilariously nonsensical account of an underground land divided into two countries – Fattypuffs and Thinifers, representing the place where fat and slim people live. The two have been at war with each other for many years, but the situation changes with the arrival of two brothers, Edmund the lump and Terry the thin, who from the 'surface' or real world interfere in their world. André Maurois has used these two opposites to show readers the absurdity of war and the advantage of living in peace and harmony with one another. The story offers endless possibilities for discussion in the classroom around the subject of politics and international conflicts, but most of all it will be enjoyed for its ingenious plot and zany characterisation. Fritz Wegner's line illustrations play an indispensable part in bringing this story alive. The book was first published in the UK in 1941 and it has been out of print for many years but thankfully Jane Nissen Books has republished it so that a new audience of readers can enjoy it. The translation is superb and it reads fluently and with ease. Although a classic in its own right, the story is not well-known among contemporary readers and therefore it has been included in this section rather than just being mentioned earlier on in the article on classics.

The Crane

Reiner Zimnik

Translated from German by Nina Ignatowicz and F.N. Monjo
New York Review Books (2004) HB £10.00 ISBN: 1 59017 075 X

Reiner Zimnik was a Polish emigrant who wrote and illustrated this book in 1970, inspired by the huge numbers of cranes that he had seen throughout Germany after the end of the Second World War. The story is about a crane that has been built at the edge of a town, and a man with a blue cap who has been appointed as a craneman; the crane is a giant and the craneman is his heart. The poetic narrative is peppered with eccentric characters such as Lektro, the craneman's friend, and an eagle that teaches the craneman how to draw a trumpet. Zimmik's book, translated from German, is one in a series of vintage children's books that have been brought back into print in handsome hardback editions by New York Review Books for the delight of contemporary readers and collectors.

'We loved the sound of these different languages, and thought the books would be a good way in which to introduce the idea of Europe' Neal Hoskins

Hello, Sailor

André Sollie, illustrated by Ingrid Godon

Translated from Dutch
Macmillan Children's Books (2003) PB £4.99 ISBN: 0 333 99290 3

Matt the lighthouse keeper watches that everything is safe out at sea, but mostly he waits for the return of his friend Sailor who has promised to return to take him off round the world. Every day his friends Rose and Felix bring Matt's food, and his post. Matt invites them to his birthday party, together with his friend Emma, who has knitted him a jumper for when he and Sailor go round the world together. But Matt is only interested in whether Sailor will return, and when he does they disappear without a word, to start their travels. A poignant little tale of friendship between two men, and their commitment to each other which overrides all other friendships, it is delicately handled and with illustrations which add layers of extra information to the text itself. A pity that it was decided to use this title, which has overtones for English readers.

Dragon Rider

Cornelia Funke

Translated from German by Anthea Bell
The Chicken House (2004) HB £12.99 ISBN: 1 903434 90 4

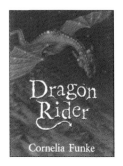

Threatened by the approach of humans who will destroy the dragons' colony, a young dragon called Firedrake embarks on an amazing journey in search of a magical place. The Rim of Heaven, according to legend, is a place where dragons can live peacefully and free from all danger. Firedrake, his brownie friend Sorrel and an orphaned boy, Ben, encounter all kinds of mythical creatures – elves, mountain dwarves and friendly humans – on a fantastical adventure that will change their lives forever. Their biggest threat is Nettlebrand, a heartless monster from the past, who wants to destroy all the silver dragons. Another imaginative fantasy by best-selling author, Cornelia Funke. The wonderful narrative style will engage any young reader and drag them inside the story to become part of this magical quest, full of exciting encounters and humorous moments. An ideal book for any fantasy lover.

The Flowing Queen

Kai Meyer

Translated from German by Anthea Bell
Egmont Children's Books (2005) HB £12.99 ISBN: 1 4052 1638 7

The people of Venice and the lagoons have always been protected by the power of the Flowing Queen – until now! Captured Mermaids pull gondolas on the lagoon while flying stone lions patrol the skies overhead and the armies of the Egyptian Empire are camped across the water where they have laid siege to the city for over 30 years. As Merle and Junipa speed across the water on their way to the 'Outcasts Canal', they have no idea what lies in store for them at the house of the master mirror-maker, Arcimboldo. Merle carries a magic water mirror that holds secrets that she doesn't fully understand. When she becomes caught up in an adventure with Serafin, from the rival Master Weaver's apprentices, it sets her off on an extraordinary journey. This is the first part of a trilogy by Kai Meyer and it is a beautifully crafted novel with poetic language and rich descriptions that really capture the magic of Venice. A best-seller in Germany, this novel promises to be popular with all fantasy lovers in the UK. Look out for the sequel, *The Stone Light*, also to be published by Egmont.

Dog
Daniel Pennac

Translated from French by Sarah Adams
Walker Books (2002) PB £4.99 ISBN: 0 7445 9009 4

Nearly drowned at birth because he is ugly, Dog spends his early life living on a rubbish tip. He is adopted by Black Nose, a bitch who advises him on how to survive the dangers of life on the streets, but when Black Nose dies unexpectedly, Dog finds himself alone. After a series of misfortunes he ends up in a dog pound. Eventually, he is rescued by 'Mr Muscle' and 'Mrs Squeak' and their daughter Plum. Although Plum is initially very fond of her new pet, she soon loses interest, and Dog suffers loneliness and a lack of affection. He runs away and makes a new life until he is reunited with Plum again. Dog works hard to train her to care for him but his adventures are not over yet! Daniel Pennac conveys his own experience of dog ownership in the epilogue, 'When you choose to live with a dog it is for life'. This is a captivating account of the life of a dog, beautifully narrated, full of suspense and a must for all dog lovers! The translation by Sarah Adams captures the fluent colloquial style.

Eye of the Wolf
Daniel Pennac, Illustrated by Max Grafe

Translated from French by Sarah Adams
Walker Books (2002) PB £4.99 ISBN: 0 7445 9010 8

There is a dreamlike quality about this novel emphaised by the powerful, unusual opening of a boy standing motionless as he stares at a wolf in a zoo. Although born worlds apart, as they look at each other they gradually establish a silent but profound telepathic channel of communication that allows them to share their very different experiences. The wolf from Alaska has lost nearly everything including an eye and his beloved pack. By rescuing his golden-furred sister whom the hunters were after, he is caught and ends up in the zoo. The boy too, has lost much and seen many terrible things as he wandered through different regions of Africa. Both wolf and boy have had to learn about life through experiencing loss and tragedy. The narrative is full of evocative descriptive detail and master storyteller Daniel Pennac weaves a tale that is both magical and mysterious. The ecological message is underplayed, yet is clear in the closing pages of the book. Sarah Adams won the 2005 *Marsh Award for Children's Literature in Translation* for her translation of this strange and highly original story about suffering, courage and growing friendship.

Kamo's Escape
Daniel Pennac

Translated from French by Sarah Adams
Walker Books (2004) PB £4.99 ISBN 0 7445 8353 5

Kamo is a sensitive, funny crazy boy who goes to spend the summer holidays with his friend's family in the Alps. Kamo has an intuitive instinct that something bad will happen to him if he rides a bike. Even the classic bike that belonged to his friend's grandfather, with its chrome mudguards and bullet marks dating back to the Second World War, cannot persuade him. Kamo's bad feeling turns out to be right. A terrible accident in the backstreets of Paris leaves him in a coma. As he lies in his hospital bed, he appears to his two friends, the narrator and Big Louis, to be someone else – someone fierce and strong. A parallel story of survival is acted out in Kamo's dream and his friends become deeply involved in helping him to survive. *Kamo's Escape* forms part of a hugely popular series about a young Parisian boy by Daniel Pennac. Intrigue about the past and an exploration of the strength of close friendship and love characterise this exquisitely crafted novel with its gentle humour captured perfectly in the translation by Sarah Adams.

Duel
David Grossman

Translated from Hebrew by Betsy Rosenberg
Bloomsbury Children's Books (1999) PB £4.99 ISBN: 0 7475 4093 4

In the margin of the letter there were three words written in red ink – 'Honour of Death'. So began an unusual story of the friendship between twelve-year-old David and the elderly Mr Rosenthal. When David reads the letter from the bully of Heidelburg University, accusing Mr Rosenthal of being 'a miserable old thief', he is full of trepidation for his friend. Somehow David must solve the mystery of the 'stolen mouth' and save two men from a duel to the death. A childhood memory narrated by David as he recalls events that took place 16 years before, it is a novel of love, honour and betrayal. It explores the friendship between a boy and an old man dealing with values from a past time – because honour is something David's elderly friend considers worth dying for. This is a quirky, compassionate story by David Grossman, one of Israel's best known novelists. Betsy Rosenberg won the *Marsh Award for Children's Books in Translation* in 2001 for the translation.

From Another World
Ana Maria Machado, illustrated by Lúcia Brandão

Translated from Portuguese (Brazil) by Luisa Baeta
Groundwood Books (2005) PB ISBN: 0 88899 641 1

Together with the family of his friends, Mariano's parents decide to leave their jobs and set up their own business by buying an old Brazilian coffee plantation and turning it into an inn. The property has an annexe and it is here that the

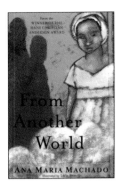

children encounter Rosario, the ghost of a young black slave girl who lived in the house many years ago. Soon the children get involved in a journey of discovery that will finally reveal the horrendous circumstances in which Rosario lost her young life. This novel explores modern Brazil as well as telling a parallel story of slavery in the 1800s. There is a glossary of terms at the end of the book, which enables the reader to become familiar with Brazilian food and words. Ana Maria Machado is an international author who has made a major contribution to children's literature, although no English translations of her books are published in the UK. In this respect this book is a welcome addition to any private or library collection.

Dreaming in Black and White

Reinhardt Jung

Translated from German by Anthea Bell
Mammoth (Egmont Children's Books) (2000) PB £3.99 ISBN: 0 7497 4157 0

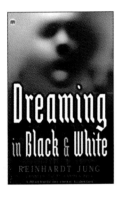

'There are dreams you can't switch off. I used to be sorry I couldn't get back into my dreams. Now I'm afraid of what's sure to happen next'. In his dreams, Hannes is transported back to 1930s Nazi Germany. Because of his physical disability he is singled out for persecution, first in the form of bullying from some of his fellow pupils, and secondly by the over-zealous Nazi teacher, Mr Lang, who follows rigidly the Nazi doctrine laid down by the Third Reich: the persecution of the Jews and the refusal to tolerate imperfection. Hannes finds solace in the unquestioning love of his mother and Hilde, his Jewish friend. However, his father is swayed by the Nazi propaganda and is prepared to sign the crucial papers that will seal Hannes' fate. This is a thought-provoking short novel that deals eloquently with the 'euthanasia' programme used by the Nazis to eliminate any social misfit and explores issues surrounding the Holocaust. A sensitively written, moving book.

I Am David

Anne Holm

Translated from Danish by L. W. Kingsland
Mammoth (Egmont Children's Books) (2000) PB £4.99 ISBN: 0 7497 0136 6

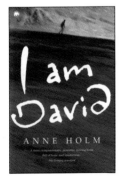

Anne Holm's 1963 account of David, a boy who has escaped from a concentration camp in an unnamed Eastern bloc country, and his search for his family, has become a classic in a genre which already contained novels of the calibre of Serraillier's *The Silver Sword*. David has survived in the camp by never allowing himself to think further than the next meal. After the death of his friend and teacher, Johannes, he never allows himself to have any affection for anyone. Ann Holm decontextualizes her character and his situation to such an extent that he stands for all dispossessed humanity, throughout time. She emphasises

both David's innate dignity and the absence of more sophisticated social skills which has resulted from his incarceration, but also portrays his gradual reassimilation into trusting relationships, which he has avoided for fear of hurt and betrayal. Although some of the coincidences which allow him to return to his (hitherto unknown) mother appear contrived, this is an intensely powerful book, of relevance to a study of the effects of ethnic cleansing in any era.

Sheep Don't Go to School
Andrew Fusek Peters (editor),
illustrated by Markéta Prachatická
Translated from Eastern European languages
Bloodaxe Books (1999) PR £5.95 ISBN: 1 85224 408 9

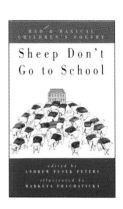

A wonderful collection of poems from eastern Europe, representing nearly two dozen countries, and spanning cultures and generations, many translated into English for the first time, by more than forty writers who have retained the indigenous spirit of the originals. There are nursery rhymes, traditional tales in verse, riddles and new poems, all of which show the readers the similarities and differences between the stories and rhymes which exist in all human experience, and which tell us, in the most entertaining ways, about life and tradition in those countries. An excellent collection for children from eastern Europe to share with their peers in British classrooms, and a powerful tool to use in emphasising the underlying interests and concerns which affect us all.

The Legend of the Fish
Gita Wolf and Sirish Rao, illustrated by Emanuele Scanziani
Tara Publications (2003) HB £12.99 ISBN: 81 86211 77 2

Following a vivid dream, Brahma, the creator, makes a perfect world from his own mind. Soon, however, he becomes unhappy with his creation – something is missing. He has created a perfect world but there is no death, and therefore no life. He asks for help from the God Vishnu, the Preserver, who is able to re-create a living world. Vishnu takes on the form of a little fish and finds a wise man, Satyavrata, to help him. Satyavrata looks after the fish and as it grows bigger and bigger he is unaware that it is the God Vishnu in disguise. Finally, the day comes when Vishnu shows himself to Satyavrata, revealing his plans for the destruction of the present world in order to create a new one. This story is a traditional Hindu tale that resembles the ancient myth of Noah's Ark, a myth that has found its parallel in cultures around the world. Impressive detailed silver and blue illustrations, silk-screened by hand on hand-made paper, complement this beautiful retelling and allow the reader into the richness of the Hindu tradition.

The Thief Lord
Cornelia Funke

Translated from German by Oliver Latsch
The Chicken House (2002) PB £5,99 ISBN: 1 903434 77 7

Two orphaned children, Prosper and Bo, are on the run, hiding amongst the labyrinth of crumbling canals and misty alleyways of Venice. Befriended by a gang of street children and their mysterious leader, the Thief Lord, they shelter in an old, disused cinema. On the boys' trail is a bungling detective, obsessed with disguises, who has been hired by their neurotic aunt to find them. The boys are drawn into a different world of street life, comradeship and adventure as they try to outwit their pursuers. However, when the Thief Lord discovers something from a forgotten past – a mysterious power that can spin time itself – this poses an even greater threat to the two boys. This is an exciting and atmospheric thriller by international best-selling author, Cornelia Funke. It is a compelling tale, rich in ingenious twists with a zany plot and well-defined characters. Oliver Latsch's translation was shortlisted for the 2005 *Marsh Award for Literature in Translation*.

Quadehar The Sorcerer (Part 1 of The Book of the Stars)
Erik L'Homme

Translated from French by Ros Schwartz
The Chicken House (2003) PB £5.99
ISBN: 1 90444 200 5

The Mystery of Lord Sha (Part 2 of The Book of the Stars)
Erik L'Homme

Translated from French by Ros Schwartz
The Chicken House (2004) PB £5.99
ISBN: 1 904442 29 3

The first two parts of a trilogy, 'The Book of the Stars', of which the final part has yet to appear in the UK, these books are, in the words of a French reader, a cross between Harry Potter and Star Wars, and have found as enthusiastic an audience in France as J.K. Rowling's hero has here. It is interesting to note that, although J.K. Rowling's French editions retain Harry's name, Erik L'Homme's young wizard has been changed from Guillemot to Robin for the benefit of UK readers, which seems to characterise the reluctance there has been to accept and translate foreign language books in the UK. Robin lives in The Lost Isle, an environmentally aware/historically regressive land cast adrift from The Real World, a representation of our own Western culture. Robin can travel between these worlds, and to The Uncertain World, a threatening world of evil creatures, both human and magical, who in turn can stray through into Robin's world. Learning his magic craft, Robin is apprenticed to Quadehar the Sorcerer, whose role seems not dissimilar to that of Rowling's Dumbledore, protective yet challenging to his pupil, while the trainee wizard searches for his father, who abandoned his family before Robin's birth to go to The Uncertain World. These books are exciting and well written, but unfortunately the immediate connection with the ancient Celtic legends to which Eric L'Homme constantly refers his French audience has been lost, and with it a layer of meaning which would lift the trilogy above the boy wizard level.

Inkheart
Cornelia Funke

Translated from German by Anthea Bell
The Chicken House (2004) PB £6.99 ISBN: 1 904442 21 8

Cornelia Funke has created a lengthy fantasy, which addresses the very essence of the reading experience. Meggie's life revolves around books, and she reads endlessly, able to select from the innumerable volumes in her home. Her only sorrow is that her father, Mo, a bookbinder, will never read aloud, fearful of his power to draw characters from their books into his own time. This he does in the case of a violent modern Italian novel, 'Inkheart', unwittingly summoning up its vicious hero, Capricorn, while at the same time losing his own wife into that novel. Cornelia Funke integrates real and realised characters into a disturbing tale of timeless vendettas played out within the modern world. She heads each chapter with a quotation from literature, usually children's, constantly reasserting the power of the written word. Throughout it all, readers empathise totally with Meggie, who, desperate to find her mother, always faces the dilemmas which reading has brought her. An absorbing, frightening and stimulating book to encourage readers to address many ethical and philosophical issues. Look out for the sequel *Inkspell* also published by Chicken House.

In the Wild
Sofia Nordin

Translated from Swedish by Maria Lundin
Groundwood Books (2005) PB ISBN: 0 88899 663 2

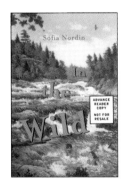

Amanda feels a social outcast and is the target of bullying. When her school organises a nature trip, Amanda dreads the thought of spending a whole week with her classmates. The white water rafting course that is supposed to be the highlight of the trip suddenly turns into a nightmare. Amanda's boat overturns in an accident and she is dragged under water by the strong current. Philip, her tormentor at school also suffers the same fate. Philip and Amanda survive and find themselves lost in the wild. The tables are now turned on Philip as he realises that he is dependent upon Amanda for her knowledge of the natural habitat that enables them to find wild edible plants to eat in order to survive. Slowly a different relationship begins to emerge as together they confront their fears. This is a thought-provoking and exciting adventure story of survival that also explores the theme of bullying and the physical and mental ability to survive, almost doubling up as a survival guide for children.

'Translation doesn't just happen in a straightforward word-for-word manner' Gillian Lathey

The Little Blue House

Sandra Comino

Translated from Spanish (Argentina) by Beatriz Hausner
and Susana Wald
Groundwood Books (2003) HB ISBN: 0 8899 503 2

In the small, remote town of Azul in rural Argentina there is a magical uninhabited little white house that once a year changes its colour to blue (azul). 12-year-old Cintia is a voracious reader and she pays frequent visits to the little house where she finds refuge. She also goes there with Bruno, her best friend and the boy she is in love with. In the little house Cintia enjoys the tranquillity and peace that she does not get at home, as her father frequently abuses her, both physically and mentally. There is also a parallel story of a young native girl who many years ago fell in love with the owner of the little house. Corruption is strongly present among the leading political figures of the town and the Mayor wants to exploit the unusual house as a tourist attraction, but most of all for his personal interest. This is a poignantly written story with strong characterisation and a cleverly constructed plot that will engage readers from beginning to end. Its subject matter – love and also abuse – would make it suitable for older children, despite the cover of the book indicating a younger audience.

The Number Devil

Hans Magnus Enzensberger,
illustrated by Rotraut Susanne Berner

Translated from German by Michael Henry Heim
Granta Books (2000) PB £12.00 ISBN: 1 86207 391 0

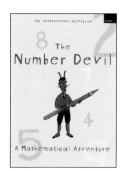

An international best-seller, this is a very interesting and innovative book that tempts children to get more involved with the many aspects of mathematics, which at first sight might appear dull or daunting. For any child showing an interest in numbers, this book is a must. 12-year-old Robert hates maths and his maths teacher. In a dreaming adventure he meets the impish Teplotaxl – the Number Devil. Through his guidance, Robert soon learns there is an easy beauty in playing with numbers and he finds that most of the stuffy mathematical theories and problems, including Pythagoras, Archimedes and other works of mathematical geniuses, can be understood in a wonderfully simple way. This is an ideal book that older children and any adult, mystified by maths, will also appreciate. To understand the full extent of what can be learnt from this book, a visit to the end section 'Seek-and-Ye-Shall-Find List' will be a positive eye opener. The translation by Michael Henry Heim uses ordinary language very effectively in a witty and helpful style, accompanied by humorous illustrations that will keep readers interested from 'The First Night' until 'The Twelfth Night'.

A Bridge to the Stars
Henning Mankell

Translated from Swedish by Laurie Thompson
Andersen Press (2005) PB £5.99 ISBN: 1 84270 439 7

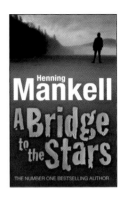

Eleven-year-old Joel is desperate to find out why his mother abandoned him and his father. Every night before he goes to sleep, he invents a story that includes her. His father means everything to him but he refuses to discuss Joel's mother, often drowning his sorrows in drink. Joel is drawn out to haunt the streets late at night by the sight of a mysterious dog. He becomes fascinated by the nocturnal activities of his neighbours – 'mad' Simon Windstorm and 'No-Nose' Gertrud and his encounter with the strange boy, Ture with whom he builds an uneasy friendship as they plan their 'Secret Society'. Joel discovers considerably more than he ever expected which helps him to understand his own family, and himself. Henning Mankell's novel is a coming-of-age tale set during the cold, dark winter nights of Northern Sweden and the descriptions of the frozen landscape are in striking contrast to the warmth of emotion that erupts between father and son. The story is loosely autobiographical, based on the author's own experience of being brought up by his father after his mother left home.

Where Were You, Robert?
Hans Magnus Enzensberger

Translated from German by Anthea Bell
Puffin Books (2001) PB £4.99 ISBN: 0 14 130680 7

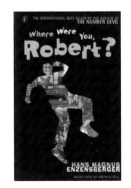

Fifteen-year-old Robert discovers that he can travel back through time. By staring at the TV screen, a film, painting or photograph his vision blurs and he enters the scene that he is looking at. A television documentary transports him to Stalin's Soviet Union in 1956, where he finds himself under suspicion of spying. As he watches a film in Moscow, he finds himself on the other side of the world in Australia in 1946. While looking at a photograph he ends up in his hometown in Germany, sixteen years earlier where he meets his grandmother as a young girl. Soon Robert is adrift in history, never sure where he will emerge next. With each journey there is a shift in time and Robert finds himself further and further away from his home and his own time. Finally he finds himself in seventeenth-century Amsterdam and can only escape by painting a picture from memory – a picture of his kitchen at home. *Where Were You, Robert?* won the *Marsh Award for Children's Literature in Translation* in 2003 for the translation by Anthea Bell.

Fly Away Home
Christine Nöstlinger

Translated from German by Anthea Bell
Andersen Press (2003) PB £5.99 ISBN: 1 84270 227 0

Austria during the last months of the Second World War; eight-year-old Christel Göth is living in Vienna under the Russian occupation. When their home is gutted by a bomb, the family – including her father who has deserted from the

army while hospitalised – take refuge in a large suburban villa just outside the city. Christel is a feisty young girl who develops a toughness that becomes a necessary part of her survival. She steals cigarettes from under the noses of the Russians for her father, explores the abandoned villas and raids their cellars for food to supply her family with, makes friends with Cohn, the Russian cook billeted with them, and even steals the Russian major's revolver! This is an autobiographical novel by Christine Nöstlinger, one of Austria's finest children's writers. It is an unsentimental account, sometimes sad, sometimes funny and although she does not dwell on gory details, nothing is evaded. It is important to read different perspectives of events that happened during the Second World War and to understand them. Eloquently translated by Anthea Bell.

Iqbal

Francesco D'Adamo

Translated from Italian by Ann Leonori
Simon and Schuster (2003) PB £7.99 ISBN: 0 689 83768 2

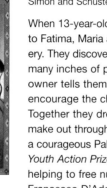

When 13-year-old Iqbal arrives at Hussain Khan's carpet factory he brings hope to Fatima, Maria and all the unseen children who are consigned to a life of slavery. They discover that their families' debt will never be cancelled, no matter how many inches of progress they make on their rugs, despite what the carpet owner tells them. It is Iqbal who is brave enough to talk about the future and encourage the children to stand together against their master's injustice. Together they dream of soaring free, high in the sky – a sky they can only just make out through their workshop window. Based on the true story of Iqbal Masih, a courageous Pakistani boy who was sold into slavery. Iqbal won the *Reebok Youth Action Prize* in 1994 for his work raising awareness of child slavery and helping to free numerous children from factories and workshops in Pakistan. Francesco D'Adamo brings Iqbal alive in this powerful and moving account of his courage and tenacity as he attempts to change the lives of thousands of Pakistani children. Although this is a tragic story, the author allows Iqbal's humanity and hope to shine through the narrative.

35 Kilos of Hope

Anna Gavalda

Translated from French by Gill Rosner
Walker Books (2004) PB ISBN: 1 84428 652 5

Thirteen-year-old Gregory hates school; he has hated it since he was four years old. Because of his constant bad marks Gregory has been kept in the same class for two years and he is eventually expelled and there is no other school that is prepared to accept him. However, Gregory is a really talented boy and his happiest moments are the ones he spends with his Grandpa Leon in his workshop, helping him and building things. Grandpa is the only one who seems to understand and encourage him. It is through his deep relationship with his grandfather that Gregory is able to find the inspiration that will allow him to overcome his physical and mental fears, when he is finally accepted in a new college. This is a thought-provoking story that brings to the surface the problem with children like Gregory, who suffer from Attention Deficit Disorder and are caught in an educational system that may not always cater to their needs. Anna Gavalda was a teacher for many years and wrote this novel for all those 'Gregorys' out there who need to be inspired.

Friday and Robinson
Michel Tournier, illustrated by Christopher Corr
Translated from French by Ralph Manheim
Walker Books (2003) PB £5.99 ISBN: 0 7445 9068 X

On the evening of the 29th of September 1759, a ship travelling to South America is wrecked in a violent storm. The only survivor, a young man called Robinson Crusoe, is dragged by the waves to a deserted island where he has to struggle to survive. After years of solitude he saves the life of an Indian, whom he names Friday. A relationship that starts as one of master and slave soon transforms into a real friendship. Michel Tournier retells the classic tale of Robinson Crusoe with a twist. The story concentrates on the development of the relationship between Friday and Crusoe, as well as the psychological development of the protagonist. Crusoe abandons his social and cultural background and gradually develops a spiritual connection with the island, with nature and, eventually, with himself. Simple black-and-white illustrations by Christopher Corr guide the reader through the story.

The Shamer's Daughter
Lene Kaaberbol
Translated from Danish by the author
Hodder Children's Books (2005) PB £5.99
ISBN: 0 340 89429 6

The Shamer's Signet
Lene Kaaberbol
Translated from Danish by the author
Hodder Children's Books (2005) PB £5.99
ISBN: 0 340 89430 X

The Serpent Gift
Lene Kaaberbol
Translated from Danish by the author
Hodder Children's Books (2005) PB £5.99
ISBN: 0 340 88363 4

The Shamer's War
Lene Kaaberbol
Translated from Danish by the author
Hodder Children's Books (2005) PB £5.99
ISBN: 0 340 88362 6

Dina has inherited the Shamer's gift from her mother – one look into her eyes and no one can mask their guilt or hide their shame. Shamers are seen as social outcasts and this makes the gift seem like a curse to eleven-year old Dina. These four novels follow the lives of the Tonerre family as they are constantly pitched into danger and adventure.

In the first book, *The Shamer's Daughter*, Dina's mother disappears after making a journey to Dunark at the request of the Dragon Lord. When she fails to return Dina must find a way to help her and Nico, the younger half brother of the evil Drakan,

whom she befriends while they are locked up in the castle dungeon. Forced to confront the vicious and revolting dragons of Dunark, Dina knows this is the only way they can escape from Drakan's clutches.

The Shamer's Signet sees Dina and her mother tricked into going with the wicked Valdracu's men and her brother, Davin, sets off in hot-headed pursuit of the man he believes, wrongly, to be responsible. Although Dina and her mother escape and a clan war is narrowly averted, the ingenious Valdracu is successful in his second attempt. Trapped and held prisoner, Dina is forced to use her gift as a weapon – if she does not, Valdracu threatens to kill her companion, a grandson of one of the clans. Davin becomes her only hope of escape.

In *The Serpent's Tail*, Dina discovers that as well as having the shamer's gift, she has inherited a far more terrifying gift – the Serpent's gift for lie and illusion – from her father, a Blackmaster. When he comes to claim his daughter, Dina and her family are catapulted into a reckless flight from their home. Her brother Davin and Nico are also in desperate danger, held in the Sagisburg by Arthos Draconis, a relative of Drakon, and Dina is finally forced to use the gift inherited from her father in order to save them.

The Shamer's War sees Davin and Dina thrown into a whirlwind adventure as they try to stop their friend Nico from following his destiny. Both are caught up in Nico's quest to take revenge on Drakon. War becomes inevitable as the clans join forces with Nico to rid themselves of the deadliest of foes. Will Dina's shamer's gift bring defeat to Nico's deadliest enemy?

Lene Kaaberbol is an excellent storyteller and translator and these Shamer novels have created an exciting world, on the edge of civilisation, magic and mystery. The harsh life of the Highlands with its rival clans and villains shows a world where those that manipulate the truth are afraid of the gifted few that can see the truth and are able to expose them.

The Prophecy of the Gems
Flavia Bujor

Translated from French by Linda Coverdale
HarperCollins Children's Books (2004) PB £5.99 ISBN: 0 00 716114 X

Jade, Opal and Amber, three 14-year-old girls from different social backgrounds, discover their fates are intertwined by an ancient prophecy that forces them to leave their homes and travel to a far-off secret kingdom called Fairyland, inhabited by magical creatures, where they must seek out Oonagh, who lives in a crystal grotto and is renowned for her wisdom. Pitted against them are the Army of Death and the evil Council of Twelve. Each girl has a quest – to reveal the power of the mystical stone that was entrusted to her and to fulfil the prophecy. Contrasted with this, is a present-day 14-year-old girl, Joa, who lies gravely ill in a Paris hospital bed. This is her dream, and the three girls' victory carries with it the secret that could return her will to live. This debut novel by a 13-year-old received a mixed reaction on publication in the UK. Linda Coverdale is an accomplished translator – having been awarded the Chevalier of the Order of Arts and Letters by France – but a few Americanisms creep into the dialogue that don't sit easily with the rest of the text.

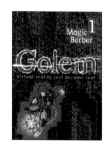

Golem 1: Magic Berber
Marie-Aude, Lorris
and Elvire Murail
Translated from French by Sarah Adams
Walker Books (2005) PB £4.99
ISBN: 1 84428 614 2

Golem 2: Joke
ISBN: 1 84428 615 0

Golem 3: Natasha
ISBN: 1 84428 616 9

Golem 4: Mr William
ISBN: 1 84428 617 7

Golem 5: Alias
ISBN: 1 8448 618 5

Twelve-year-old Majid and his fellow pupils of 8D live on the run-down Moreland estate full of immigrant families. When Majid wins a top of the range New Generation BIT Computer his world is changed forever. Knowing little about computers he asks his English teacher, Hugh Mullins, to help him. Somehow, a game known as `Golem' – where a warrior appears on screen – mysteriously manages to install itself on both computers. This is a highly addictive game, which becomes a real part of Hugh's, Majid's and his friends' lives. Strange things start to happen – electrical powercuts, computers crashing, blue smoke that is seen emerging from Majid's flat, not to mention the strange goings on in the basement of the tower block where he lives. Is Golem just an innocent game? or is there a hidden depth to it? Golem was intended as a way of passing on subliminal messages to all potential shoppers by B Corp, a supermarket conglomerate. Now the directors of B Corp want it back and are prepared to go to any lengths to get it.

This story is in the tradition of the all-action comic strip series popular in France, with much of the action taking place on a computer screen. This Golem series of cleverly written books by the Murail siblings, France's most famous literary family, have been a great success in their native country. Sarah Adams has done an outstanding job in translating the backslang used by young urban French people. She has successfully managed to transport this story from an Algerian community in France to a high-rise housing estate somewhere in Britain so that it will reach a whole new audience of UK readers. This set of tough, streetwise stories will appeal to young people who are keen on cyberspace and reluctant boy readers. It is essential to read the whole series though as they don't stand alone well as individual novels.

The Ring of the Slave Prince

Bjarne Reuter

Translated from Danish by Tiina Nunnally
Andersen Press (2004) PB £7.99 ISBN: 1 84270 370 6

It is 1639 and a storm is howling around the Caribbean island of Nevis where 14-year-old Tom O'Connor lives. Tom is determined to set his mother and half sister free from their life of servitude and every day he goes down to the sea in the hope that he will find some treasure. When he saves the lives of a shipwrecked Spaniard, Ramón the Pious, and a slave boy, Boto, who is an African prince, Ramón promises to give Tom half of the fortune that they will receive when they return the boy to his father. After Ramón tricks him, disappearing with the slave prince, Tom sets out on a journey that will change his life forever. As he travels over land and sea, working as a blacksmith, a slave overseer and a cabin boy, he experiences many kinds of adventure. This is a well-developed, thought-provoking novel with a plot full of twists and turns, action and indirect moral questions. Tom has to make a very personal journey as he develops from child to man through the knowledge he acquires – that love and friendship are more valuable than any material fortune.

Through a Glass, Darkly

Jostein Gaarder

Translated from Norwegian by Elizabeth Rokkan
Dolphin (Orion Children's Books) (2004) PB £4.99 ISBN: 1 85881 7 69 2

'You see everything in a glass, darkly' Ariel explains to Cecilia, as she lies ill in bed on Christmas Eve. Her family are valiantly making their Christmas preparations in the knowledge that Cecilia is not going to get better. Ariel is an angel and this is the first of many visits to Cecilia. He tells her that the whole of creation is a looking glass and the whole world is a mystery. As the weeks pass, through her philosophical discussions with Ariel, Cecilia's mood swings between anger and denial, hope and despair. Ariel points out to her that humans come and go, 'you are the ones who don't last . . . It's as if God is blowing bubbles with you'. Finally, she reaches a calm acceptance of her lot and prepares to leave. This is another original and moving story by Jostein Gaarder, which explores the great mystery of life and death. It has a depth and simplicity that deals with a difficult subject in a thought-provoking way.

The Last Black Cat

Eugene Trivizas

Translated from Greek by Sandy Zervas
Egmont Children's Books (2005) PB £4.99 ISBN: 1 4052 1281 0

This is the story of a black cat that lives a peaceful and happy life on an island. He has only ever had to worry about stealing fish, hanging out with fellow cats and the love of his life, Graziella. One night however, he witnesses the kidnapping of a

fellow cat. Suddenly, one by one all the black cats on the island begin mysteriously disappearing until there is only one black cat left. Behind these abductions lies a sinister society who have convinced the government that black cats bring bad luck and are responsible for the nation's problems. Eugene Trivizas has created a story that deals with discrimination as well as the power of illogical superstition seen from the perspective of a cat as the main protagonist. This book is full of imagination and original ideas. Although it can be grim reading at times, the vivid dialogue and good sense of humour that runs throughout make this an unusual novel.

The Dream Merchant
Isabel Hoving

Translated from Dutch by Hester Velmans
Walker Books (2005) HB £14.99 ISBN: 0 7445 83357

When 12-year-old Joshua receives a mysterious telephone call in the middle of the night from Gippart International, little does he realise that he is about to embark on an extraordinary journey into 'Umaya' – a place between dreams and reality. Why is an international corporation so convinced that Josh is the key to conquering their new market: the past? Together with his friends Baz and Teresa, he find himself in the middle of a nightmare. In order to find their way back, they must follow a trail that takes them through many different whirlwind adventures as they learn how to control aspects of Umaya. This is an epic time-travel fantasy – all 638 pages of it! Isabel Hoving has produced a thought-provoking debut novel that is rich in adventure, suspense and extraordinary imagination. It was first published in Holland as "The Winged Cat" and won the 2003 *Golden Kiss Award*, Holland's most prestigious children's book prize. An ambitious project for any translator, but Hester Velmans has done an excellent job of conveying this complex novel to a British setting. With its multi-layered text it is ideal for fantasy lovers who enjoy a challenging story.

The Solitaire Mystery
Jostein Gaarder, illustrated by Hilda Kramer

Translated from Norwegian by Sarah Jane Hails
Dolphin (Orion Children's Books) (2004) PB £5.99 ISBN: 1 85881 636 X

During a trip from Norway to Greece – the ancient home of Philosophers – 12-year-old Hans Thomas and his father go in search of Hans' mother who disappeared eight years before, 'to find herself'. Jostein Gaarder uses an intriguing and engaging non-nuclear family, to relate a story of worlds within worlds, as Hans struggles to understand his strife-riven family history. Set in the present and past, with a whole host of characters both real and imaginary, the story includes a magical dwarf who gives Hans a special magnifying glass so that he can read the miniature book discovered in a sticky bun, given to him by a mysterious old Baker. Each chapter is symbolised by an individual card from a pack of cards including the often forgotten Joker. The journey allows the boy and his father to engage in some homespun philosophy that involves understanding the uniqueness of life and destiny, and allows the reader to appreciate the randomness of life and the effects that the actions of today can have for future generations. This is a compelling book full of puzzles and mystery, humour and optimism, and Sarah Jane Hails' translation has captured the spirit of this unusual story.

No Roof in Bosnia

Els de Groen

Translated from Dutch by Patricia Crampton
Spindlewood Books (2001) PB £4.99 ISBN: 0 907349 22 6

NO ROOF IN BOSNIA
Els de Groen

When Aida enters the deserted village of Brodiste in Bosnia she is afraid. The war rages all around her and danger is ever present. Finding a farmhouse she encounters Antonia who lives alone with her dog, Napoleon. Gradually Aida learns to trust Antonia and she decides to stay until she can make her way safely to the coast. When Josip, Antonia's nephew, visits to get more supplies for his mountain hideout, he warns his aunt of the dangers of staying in the village. Aida joins the four teenagers hiding out in the mountains and they learn to live together despite their different ethnic backgrounds. However, disaster strikes when the Serbs capture Josip and the other two boys. Aida and Mila find themselves alone and decide to set off on their way to the Adriatic Coast where they hope to find their friends again. This novel captures the futility and heartache of ethnic intolerance together with the pain and the human consequences of not-so-distant politics. It is a powerful, compelling and realistic story of human courage and frailty in which there are no easy answers to be found.

The Ice Road

Jaap ter Haar

Translated from Dutch by Martha Mearns
Barn Own Books (2004) PB £5.99 ISBN: 1 903015 38

THE ICE ROAD
Jaap ter Haar

It is 1942 and the German army surrounds Leningrad. The citizens are being bombarded day and night, no one can get out, no food can get in and the temperature is below zero. Plans are being made to evacuate the children from the city and 12-year-old Boris Morenko's mother wants him to go too. However, the Ice Road stretches across Lake Ladoga and is the only way out of the city. Many have perished on this treacherous journey across the ice, including Boris's father. Food is strictly rationed and Boris's mother is ill. Desperate for food, Boris and his best friend Nadia take a perilous trek behind enemy lines in search of potatoes. It is a dangerous mission but the need to find food drives them on. When they receive help from an unexpected source, Boris is given a whole new perception of the war. Jaap ter Haar's novel is an uplifting and thought-provoking book that evokes the terrible hardships of the nine-hundred-day siege of Leningrad during the Second World War. It is a story of survival, bravery, friendship, compassion and the understanding that can come from shared suffering.

Malka
Mirjam Pressler

Translated from German by Brian Murdoch
Macmillan Children's Books PB £4.99 ISBN: 0 330 39990 X

Poland, 1943; seven-year-old Malka's childhood is shattered when the Germans begin their 'special operations' and she has to escape across the border to Hungary with her mother, Hannah Mai and sister, Minna. After being separated from them, Malka arrives back in Poland where she has to learn to survive alone in the Jewish ghetto and on the run, in a climate of fear and danger, while her desperate mother struggles to find her. The narrative follows the story of Hannah Mai as she searches for her youngest daughter and of Malka as she fends off starvation and the regular round-up of the Jews. Mirjam Pressler's narrative conveys the brutality and harshness of Malka's life without sensationalising it. Both poignant, and at times shocking – in particular, how some of her own community shun her when she needs their help most – but there are many individual acts of kindness that are heart-warming in this powerful, haunting novel that is based on a true story.

Daniel Half Human
David Chotjewitz

Translated from German by Doris Orgel
Simon and Schuster (2005) PB £5.99 ISBN: 0 689 87295 X

The persecution of the Jews in Germany before and during the Second World War has been previously featured in countless books aimed at young people, but in *Daniel Half Human* the subject is presented from a different perspective. Daniel believes himself to be Aryan, but then he finds out that his mother is Jewish, making him half Jewish and therefore half human in the eyes of the 'supreme' Aryan race. This discovery causes an enormous amount of psychological upheaval for Daniel, particularly as his best friend Armin is an active member of the Hitler Youth. He is being indoctrinated by the system to hate the Jews and later discovers the truth about Daniel, that will test their friendship to the limit. David Chotjewitz, through his main character Daniel, skillfully conveys the absurdity of the hatred of Jews in Germany during the 1930s before the outbreak of war. This is a powerful novel, difficult to put down, which has been poignantly written and beautifully translated. This is an important contribution to anti-Semitism and Second World War literature for adolescents.

The Final Journey
Gudrun Pausewang

Translated from German by Patricia Crampton
Puffin Books (1998) PB £4.99 ISBN: 0 14 037800 6

This was the first of Gudrun Pausewang's novels about Jewish life under the Nazi regime to appear in the UK. 11-year-old Alice has been in hiding for the last three years, for fear she and her grandparents will be rounded up and transported to camps like her Jewish friends and relatives. When the soldiers finally come for them, Alice must endure a long and terrible journey to the concentration camp, together with a journey towards maturity, in which she discovers the truth about her parents, about the elaborate subterfuge with which her grandfather has tried to shield her from reality, the compassion, courage and inhumanity of others who are competing for their very existence, and her own capacity for these qualities. Winner of the *Marsh Award for Children's Literature in Translation* in 1999, Gudrun Pausewang's short novel protects readers from nothing, neither the confusion of emotions among the prisoners nor the appalling indignity of the situation, in which love, life and death all happen in fear and squalor, nor the final terrible outcome. Compelling and deeply moving.

Traitor
Gudrun Pausewang

Translated from German by Rachel Ward
Andersen Press (2004) PB £5.99 ISBN: 1 84270 313 7

Gudrun Pausewang's novel contradicts the popular perception that all Germans were Nazis, and therefore evil, and that all Germans knew of the atrocities being committed in the name of the Fatherland. Anna lives in a remote village where the population is part German, part Czech, the former, in varying degrees, supporting Nazi ideology, the latter equally varied in the degree of their opposition to Hitler's cause. During the closing months of the Second World War, Anna stumbles upon a fugitive – a Russian and enemy – in her family's barn. Though her brother Felix accepts the Nazi propaganda unquestioningly, Anna cannot, and she sees each human being for themselves, even if they are 'enemies'. Her dilemma is searingly portrayed, and is painfully obvious to readers: the views of the fervent Nazis in the village, including her uncle, are pitted against those of her grandmother, whose religious beliefs cannot allow Hitler to supplant God. Constantly questioning the individual's role, the novel's shocking ending with its dreadful denouncement underlines the futility of war. An incredibly moving book, which will draw readers into Anna's agonised decision making.

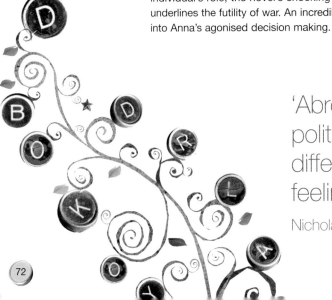

'Abroad is not just about politics; it is also about different ways of seeing, feeling and behaving'

Nicholas Tucker

Brothers
Ted van Lieshout

Translated from Dutch by Lance Salway
CollinsFlamingo/HarperCollins Children's Books (2001) PB £4.99 ISBN: 0 00 711231 9

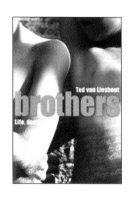

This short but powerful novel examines a number of issues, which will resonate with adolescent boys. Luke has lost his younger brother Marius to a wasting sickness. Writing in the unused pages in his brother's diary, Luke revisits his relationship with him, considers his parents' effect on the lives of the brothers, and wonders if brotherhood can survive death. Through this soliloquy he examines his brother's sexuality, overtly heterosexual, but covertly and passionately homosexual, and through it his own early feelings for older men. Empowered by the realisation that he must be true to his own feelings, Luke finally announces to his parents that he too is gay, and is reassured by their support and the reaffirmation of their love for him. Shortlisted for the *Marsh Award for Children's Literature in Translation*, 2003, this is a sensitive but unflinching translation by Lance Salway of Ted Van Lieshout's text which examines life, death and truth, and which also offers young adults strategies for coping with the death of a sibling.

Dance of the Assassins
Hervé Jubert

Translated from French by Anthea Bell
Hodder Children's Books (2004)
PB £6.99 ISBN: 0 340 87538 0

Devil's Tango
Hervé Jubert

Translated from French by Anthea Bell
Hodder Children's Books (April 2005)
PB £6.99 ISBN: 0 340 87540 2

Dance of the Assassins is set in the future, where technological advances have meant that for generations the city of Basle – with its amazing virtual reality replica historical cities – has been a crime-free zone. However, when a gruesome murder takes place in a dark alley of Victorian London, it has all the hallmarks of Jack the Ripper! Roberta Morgenstern, a qualified witch from the Academy of Sorcery and her assistant, Clément Martineau, a recent graduate from the police academy, are assigned the task of solving the murder. In order to find out who is resurrecting some of history's most notorious murderers, they must trace the steps of a criminal mastermind. This leads them through a number of virtual eras from 19th Century London, 17th Century Paris of Louis XIV and Renaissance Venice to Montezuma's Mexico, where they find themselves having an assignation with the Devil himself.

The Devil's Tango sees the detective duo once again negotiate the dangers of another spate of terrible and violent crimes that are taking place in Basle. The city is also experiencing incessant rain and the water levels are slowly rising. Soon the dams will be breached and all of Basle will be underwater. Morgenstern and

Martineau are on the trail of the mysterious Baron of the Mists who appears to be leaving a trail of destruction in his wake. With the help of the Queen of the Gypsies and the pirates of the lagoon they set out to stop the terrible calamity that will befall Basle.

These books are imaginative, dark and complex with their mix of graphic novel, historical and detective fictional influences. They are a compelling read with some ingenious plotting and plenty of twists that at times can be difficult to follow. The darkness is counteracted by humour and some endearing characters. Hervé Jubert is a gifted and exciting new writer full of inventiveness and both books are beautifully translated by Anthea Bell. Challenging novels, full of theatrical flourish, they will appeal to older readers, especially boys.

Falling
Anne Provoost

Translated from Dutch by John Nieuwenhuizen
Allen and Unwin (1997) PB £5.99 ISBN: 186448 444 6

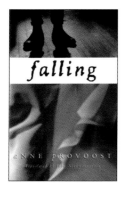

After the death of his grandfather, Lucas and his mother are spending the summer in his house near a French country town. As the long, oppressive summer progresses Lucas becomes aware of a dark secret surrounding his grandfather's activities during the Second World War. Oblique references are made about the fate of some local Jewish children and Lucas begins to feel that he is in some way responsible for his grandfather's actions. Meanwhile, racial tension is growing in the neighbourhood against the Arab migrant population. Lucas falls increasingly under the spell of Benoît, a smooth-talking right-wing extremist who draws him into violent action against the migrant workers. And then there is enigmatic Caitlin with her strong opinions, who challenges Lucas' views. When tragedy strikes he is forced to make a terrible choice, and risk repeating his grandfather's mistakes. This is a dark and deeply disturbing book that deals with the seductive power of extreme nationalism, Holocaust denial and racial intolerance as it follows Lucas' journey from innocence and ignorance to a gradual understanding of himself and his family's past.

Good for Nothing
Michel Nöel

Translated from French by Shelley Tanaka
Groundwood Books (2004) PB ISBN: 0 88899 616 0

Set in 1959, this is the story of 15-year-old Nipishish, a young Metis – of mixed American Indian and French Canadian ancestry – who returns to his reserve in northern Quebec after having been expelled from his residential school. Back on his reserve he is still unhappy as he feels it has nothing to offer him. He is sent to a new school in town where he has to reside with a foster family. Nipishish finds it difficult to fit in with the white people of the town and begins to become aware of the discrimination against Indians, although he is, himself, of mixed race. Rescued by his Indian family from life in the city, he returns to the reserve, where

he finally discovers his own identity as an Indian and he starts to fight for his rights and confront the laws that are imposed on the Indians by the white people. Over a period of two years Nipishish develops from an innocent teenager to a conscious and courageous young man who is determined to represent his whole community. A very thought-provoking novel, based on real incidents of racism and discrimination that the native people have endured in Quebec.

In the Shadow of the Ark
Anne Provoost

Translated from Dutch by John Nieuwenhuizen
Simon and Schuster (2004) HB £12.99 ISBN: 0 689 87269 0

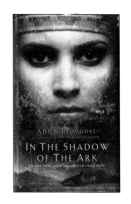

The rising waters in the Marsh Lands have forced Re Jana and her family to flee their home and settle in the desert that has now been transformed into a tented city bustling with industry. Her father is a boat builder and they set up camp alongside the shipyard where a giant boat is being constructed. Rumours of an impending flood seem too remote to be believable in a land where water is scarce. The Builder, an ailing, autocratic and stubborn old man, follows the commands of his God the 'Unnameable', who is a demanding deity. Despite falling in love with Ham, the Builder's son, Re Jana questions everything that she hears. As the skies darken and the deluge finally begins, panic spreads throughout the gathering tribes as the doors to the ark are finally sealed. Anne Provoost has spun a dark, elegantly written epic, set in the apocalyptic days of Noah's ark. The detailed descriptions of the building of the ark are masterly and John Nieuwenhuizen's translation captures the rich tapestry of this story. This is a book that can be appreciated by older readers and adults as well.

Letters from the Living
Kazumi Yumoto

Translated from Japanese by Cathy Hirano
Floris Books (2003) PB £4.99 ISBN: 0 86315 385 2

Six-year-old Chiaki lives in Japan with her mother. When her father dies she has to deal with her grief alone as her mother is too distracted and fails to communicate with her. When they move to Poplar House, a new relationship gradually develops between Chiaki and the scary landlady, Mrs Yanagi, who tells her that she has been given a divine mission, to carry 'letters to the dead' when she herself dies. Chiaki starts writing letters to her father that she hopes will help her to come to terms with her loss and entrusts them to Mrs Yanagi. When the old lady dies many years later, Chiaki, now a young woman, comes back to attend her funeral and begins a journey into the past as she learns the truth about her father's death and starts to understand the sense of her own life. Kazumi Yumoto's narrative explores the many different aspects of Japanese life and culture. An unusual book that focuses on the effect that the loss of a parent has on a young child and her relationship with her mother as they struggle to come to terms with it.

Loves Me Loves Me Not

Per Nilsson

Translated from Swedish by Tara Chace
Hodder Children's Books (2005) PB £5.99 ISBN: 0 340 88442 8

A 16-year-old Swedish boy sits alone in his room surrounded by all the objects collected from a short-lived relationship with 'Heart's Delight' – a beautiful red-haired girl whom he met on a bus. Gradually, one by one, he destroys all the items that are connected with Ann-Katrin – he tears up his bus pass from their first meeting, drops the pot plant of lemon balm she gave him over the edge of the balcony. A record that contained his favourite song is thrown in the air like a frisbee and the Swiss army knife goes over the balcony too. The novel is cleverly set out like a film that has been edited and re-shot, scene by scene. As he plays the film of his past over and over in his head, memory and reality blend into one story, the final showing. This is a bitter-sweet story about first love and heartbreak. An ideal coming-of-age book for young boys, the narrative is short and sharp conveying all the emotions that the boy goes through as he struggles to make sense of everything and finally move on with his life.

Mimus

Lilli Thal

Translated from German by John Brownjohn
Allen and Unwin (2005) PB £6.99 ISBN: 1 74114 702 6

After years of merciless war between the kingdoms of Vinland and Moltovia, King Philip has gone to celebrate the signing of the peace treaty at the court of his former enemy, King Theodo. Twelve-year-old Prince Florin has been lured into joining his father, but what greets him is a macabre betrayal. His father and loyal advisors have been tricked and imprisoned in the squalid dungeons of Theodo's castle. A different kind of humiliation awaits Florin, when he is apprenticed to Mimus, the enigmatic and unpredictable court jester. Living in a stable and half starved, he is forced to train to play the fool and perform in front of the King and his court. Florin despairs until he learns of a daring rescue plot, but the stakes are high and the fate of his father hangs in the balance. This is an excellent medieval adventure full of suspense enlivened by Mimus' clever and witty repartee. Although the setting is fictitious, through beautiful prose, Lilli Thal succeeds in accurately evoking life during the Middle Ages. Mimus is a multi-layered novel that deals with hatred and revenge, courage and friendship, humour and forgiveness. John Brownjohn's translation captures the atmosphere of the medieval court and the jester's comedy perfectly.

The Orange Girl
Jostein Gaarder

Translated from Norwegian by James Anderson
Weidenfeld and Nicolson (2004) HB £9.99 ISBN: 0 297 84904 2

Georg, the 15-year-old narrator has been given a – 'letter to the future' from his father, who died when he was four years old. His father tells him the story of the Orange Girl – a mysterious and beautiful young woman he encountered on a tram in Oslo while a student. Also woven into the letter is his father's curiosity about the Hubble Space Telescope and whether it has revealed any more secrets of the universe. What does emerge from this short novel, encapsulated in the letter from father to son, is the picture of a young man in love with life and the universe, who learns that he is dying and that his time is running out. Georg comes to realise that the Hubble Telescope is a metaphor for his father's letter to the child he will never see grow up. When Georg discovers the identity of the Orange Girl he begins to understand why his father believed the story was so important. A poignant story with contrasting parts – the 'fairy tale story' of The Orange Girl and the Hubble Telescope, around which are framed philosophical questions of existence.

Secrets in the Fire
Henning Mankell

Translated from Swedish by
Anne Connie Stuksrud
Allen and Unwin (2000) PB £5.99
ISBN: 1 86508 181 7

Playing With Fire
Henning Mankell

Translated from Swedish
by Anna Paterson
Allen and Unwin (2002) PB £5.99
ISBN: 1 86508 714 9

In *Secrets in the Fire* Sofia and her family flee from their home in rural Mozambique after bandits destroy their village and kill most of the inhabitants, including her father. Desperately poor, they attempt to start afresh, but the dangers of war are ever present. Sofia is forced to rebuild her life when she and her sister, Maria, are involved in a landmine explosion that has devastating consequences – her sister is killed and she loses both her legs.

Playing with Fire continues with the story of Sofia and her family. When Sofia's beautiful sister Rosa succumbs to a mysterious illness, she is eventually diagnosed with AIDS. There are no drugs available, no hospital treatment and no counselling to help Rosa. Sofia and her mother, Lydia, struggle to support the family and, in their different ways, to help Rosa come to terms with her illness and its inevitable consequences. For Sofia, her sister's terrible illness is yet another blow, but throughout it all her courage remains steadfast. This is based on a true story of a young girl living in war-torn Mozambique. Pitted against incredible adversity Sofia's courage manages to shine through as she comes to terms with her terrible disability and transcends the brutality and horror that has shattered her childhood. Henning Mankell is best known for his detective novels, but these important books, delivered in spare, unsentimental language, provide teenage readers with an understanding of the issues of landmines and the AIDS epidemic.

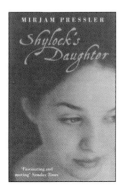

Shylock's Daughter
Mirjam Pressler

Translated from German by Brian Murdoch
Macmillan Children's Books (2001) PB £4.99 ISBN: 0 330 48410 9

Set in Venice in 1568, Mirjam Pressler's novel subsists within the framework of Shakespeare's play *The Merchant of Venice*. Sixteen-year-old Jessica is tired of the endless restrictions of the Jewish Ghetto and of her father Shylock's meanness. She has fallen in love with the handsome, charming aristocratic Lorenzo and now she wants to be free. However, the price of freedom is desperately high because Lorenzo is a Christian and Jessica a Jew. The ambiguities of the play are explored and developed and some of the actual dialogue, especially Shylock's words, takes the form of direct quotations from the play. Dalilah, Shylock's foster-daughter, is an important new character and several chapters are narrated directly from Dalilah's perspective. Venetian ghetto life is portrayed with historical accuracy and the author explores the plight of the Jews in a society where racism exists and cultures clash. The significance of Jessica's feisty decision to turn her back on her religion and her family is brought into devastating focus in this powerful novel that is well written and beautifully characterised. Praise must go to the translator, Brian Murdoch who has captured the text so faithfully.

Sophie's World
Jostein Gaarder

Translated from Norwegian by Paulette Møller
Dolphin (Orion Children's Books) (2003) PB £5.99 ISBN: 1 85881 530 4

Why does Sophie keep receiving postcards addressed to a girl called Hilde? And who is the mysterious philosopher that appears from nowhere and is sending her envelopes asking such questions as 'Who are You?' as well as detailed lessons in philosophy? However, nothing is what it seems. With complex twists and turns, Jostein Gaarder weaves a wonderfully original and engaging mystery story that also forms a completely accessible introduction to philosophy and philosophers from ancient Greece through hundreds of years of philosophy to the late twentieth century. It is an ideal novel to draw teenagers into the world of philosophy as it raises profound questions about the meaning of life and the origins of the universe With an ingenious subtext, this novel will absorb any reader as they are invited to contemplate life and the complexities of existence. Translating this book is no mean feat and Paulette Møller has done an excellent job of conveying these often very complex concepts. There is a useful 'Notes of Philosophers' section at the back of the book.

Summer with Mary-Lou
Stefan Casta

Translated from Swedish by Tom Geddes
Andersen Press (2005) PB £5.99 ISBN: 1 84270 246 7

As 14-year-old Adam turns the corner in a busy Stockholm street, he bumps into Mary-Lou, an old childhood friend. Adam is planning to spend the summer in the family cottage by the lake and invites Mary-Lou to go with him. As children they had often spent summer holidays together, until tragedy struck when Mary-Lou had a terrible accident that confined her to a wheelchair. No one really knows what happened that day – whether she jumped or fell – but she has never spoken about it since. As Adam and Mary-Lou spend their first summer together since the accident they slowly rebuild their friendship and over the weeks, learn through each other to come to terms with their own inner turmoil. Adam tries to capture the real Mary-Lou – hidden behind the steely iciness – on paper as he draws her portrait. Through beautiful prose, Stefan Casta provides a novel full of atmospheric descriptions together with affectionate humour as Adam tries to help Mary-Lou come to terms with her disability.

When I was a Soldier: One Girl's real Story
Valérie Zenatti

Translated from French by Adriana Hunter
Bloomsbury Children's Books (2005) PB £5.99 ISBN: 0 7475 7566 5

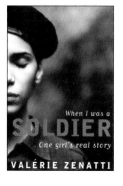

This is a fascinating true story of a young girl's experience of her two years' national service in the Israeli Defence Army (IDF). At the age of 18, Valérie is thrust into an alien world as she becomes soldier 3810159 and has to learn to adapt to the structured order of military life. It is a strange existence, crushingly strict routines, gruelling marches, and plenty of latrine, kitchen and guard duty. She is trained to defend her country and learns to fire a weapon, despite the fact that women in the IDF do not go into combat. Although Valérie enjoys her training in intelligence work she begins to question the use of arms and the reality of life for the Palestinians living under Israeli occupation. This is a funny, perceptive novel that paints an illuminating portrait of a young woman growing up in a society where violent conflict is accepted as part of every day normal life. Credit must go to the book's translator, Adriana Hunter, for conveying the author's 'teenage voice' as she recounts her story.

Epileptic
David B.

Translated from French
Jonathan Cape (2005) HB £16.99 ISBN: 0 224 07502 0

This is an autobiographical account told in graphic novel format. It is an original and poignant account of a young boy trying to come to terms with the changes to family life after his older brother, Jean-Christophe, is diagnosed as an epileptic. Through stories and pictures, it describes how his parents and family adjust to Jean-Christophe's condition and their struggle to overcome his disability. The book is also a social account, as perceived through the eyes of a young boy, of growing up in France in the 1960s. David B. is one of Europe's most important and innovative comic-strip artists. This novel is based upon his own experience of learning to cope with his brother's condition through his fantastic drawings of battle scenes which are a reflection of his inner turmoil; it is an incredible piece of work that can be moving and shocking at times but told with honesty and pathos. This is the first translation of all six volumes. It is a modern classic in its own right, which offers parents as well as children an insight into the experience of living with epilepsy.

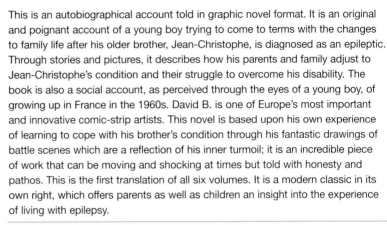

Persepolis: The Story of A Childhood
Marjane Satrapi

Translated from French
Jonathan Cape (2003) HB £12.99
ISBN: 0 224 06440 1

Persepolis 2: The Story of A Return
Marjane Satrapi

Translated from French by Anjali Singh
Jonathan Cape (2004) HB £12.99
ISBN: 0 224 07440 7

Here in the UK readers are not used to the graphic novel genre and sometimes we still have archaic and old-fashioned attitudes towards these types of books. This is not the case in France and the neighbouring Low Countries where comics and graphic novels have been part of daily life for many years and are read by both children and adults alike. From France come two of the best graphic novels of recent years first published in 2000 and 2001 respectively, although the author and illustrator is Iranian by birth and now settled in France. These two books are a moving, poignant autobiographical account of Marjane Satrapi's childhood in Iran during the Islamic Revolution and the war with Iraq. *Persepolis: The Story of A Childhood* is seen through the eyes of Marjane, living with her liberally minded parents, through major social and political change as the fundamentalist regime is ushered in. At the start of the story, Marjane is six years old and the reader is able to follow the effects that these changes have on her family and school life. The cartoon-type illustrations, although simplistic at first sight, superbly convey humour, emotions and ideas with black and white images that are full of expression but without being over sentimental.

Persepolis 2: The Story of A Return covers the life of the young protagonist after she leaves Iran and settles in Vienna. It movingly depicts her efforts to overcome loneliness, her cultural identity crisis and the strong influence of the past on her present new life and ends with her return to Iran after graduation.

Linnea in Monet's Garden

Christina Björk, illustrated by Lena Anderson

Translated from Swedish by Joan Sandin
R&S Books (1987) HB £6.95 ISBN: 91 29 58314 4

Linnea is a young girl who loves flowers and goes to visit the flat of her neighbour, old Mr Bloom. Mr Bloom used to be a gardener and in his library he has a book about Monet with pictures of his garden of water lilies and his paintings. Linnea is so taken by the book that she wants to find out more about the artist and his work. Mr Bloom then suggests a trip to Paris, France to visit Monet's place of birth and the museums where his paintings are exhibited. Using two fictional characters, an adult and a child, the author is able to tell children about Monet's life and also explain his work in a way that they can relate to and understand. Besides the colour illustrations of our two fictional characters there are black and white and colour illustrations throughout of Monet and his paintings. At the end of the book there is a list of museums in Paris with suggestions of things to do in the city as well as a timeline of Monet's life. Even though *Linnea in Monet's Garden* was published in the 1980s it is still a best-selling book which maintains its original appeal. This is a friendly and innovative way of introducing well-known artists and art to children.

Vendela in Venice

Christina Björk, illustrated by Inga-Karin Eriksson

Translated from Swedish by Patricia Crampton
R&S Books (1999) HB £11.99 ISBN: 91 29 64559 X

Vendela and her father have been reading and doing some research about Venice. To satisfy Vendela's curiosity dad proposes that they go and visit this magical city. The book is divided into short chapters, each one dealing in chronological order with the events that take place during their stay, starting with their arrival at the airport, a vaporetto journey to the hotel, a visit to the famous Floriani café, the visits to museums and their final departure back to Stockholm. The book has a fictional rather than a factual, non-fictional feel thanks to all the dialogue between the young girl and her father about the places that they visit. *Vendela in Venice* is an ideal book to introduce a well-known tourist destination to young children. Fully illustrated in colour with plenty of samples of Venetian art, architecture and famous landmarks, it also contains a useful list of 'things you might like to know about Venice', including information on gondolas, painters, museums, as well as practical information such as Italian language hints and shopping. This book encourages young children to find out more and learn about other cultures in a friendly and easy-to-read style.

Who Can Crack the Leonardo da Vinci Code?
Thomas Brezina, illustrated by Laurence Sartin

Translated from German by Hannah Sartin
Prestel (2005) PB £9.99 ISBN: 3 7913 3426 3

Thomas Brezina, a prolific and popular author in continental Europe, has devised a children's adventure game book which was inspired by Dan Brown's *The Da Vinci Code*. Accompanied by a little dog called Pablo, readers start their journey in a Museum of Adventures where they travel back in time to meet the artist himself and are guided through his paintings and scientific works. Using the Book of Riddles, a mirror and the hieroglyphic scroll provided, readers can solve seven riddles hidden inside the paintings, and discover the secret that will save the museum from cunning villains. The reproductions of Leonardo's works and Laurence Sartin's line drawings enliven a fairly wordy text, in which pictures by other famous artists are also encountered. An unusual way to intro duce children to an intriguing artist, which should tempt them to explore deeper into his life and times, and those of other artists. Watch out for the next title in this series, *Who Can Save Vincent's Hidden Treasure?*

The London Jungle Book
Bhajju Shyam

Translated from (the oral) Hindi by Sirish Rao and Gita Wolf
Tara Publications (2005) HB £9.99 ISBN: 81 86211 87 X

Bhajju Shyam comes from the tribal village of Patangath in central India. He was commissioned to decorate the walls of a restaurant in Islington, London and this book is the result of his two months' experience of living and working in the city and his personal views of people, places and customs. Through his paintings he manages to give an interpretation which is closely associated with the Gond art of his home region. This book successfully brings together the two different cultures through expressive folk paintings, with the added bonus of having the artist himself explaining each piece of artwork and, in doing so, placing it in its wider cultural context. *The London Jungle Book* has not been translated from a Hindi written text, but the editors interviewed the artist – who does not speak English – and then transferred onto paper his cultural experiences for the delight of young people and adults alike. The Gond ethnic illustrations are highly expressive and beautifully manage to put across the feelings of the artist. Particularly effective are those of the London under-ground system represented by snakes and Big Ben merging with a giant rooster, also featured on the front cover.

Under the Spell of the Moon: Art for Children from the World's Great Illustrators

Foreword by Katherine Paterson

Edited by Patricia Aldana
Texts translated by Stan Dragland
Groundwood Books (2004) HB ISBN: 088899 559 8

This beautifully produced book shows the amazing talent of many children's book illustrators throughout the world. The artists were commissioned to illustrate a text of their choice. They have selected nursery rhymes, songs, poems or prose from their own childhood which have then been illustrated in their own style. The text has been written in their own language, which has been translated into English by Stan Dragland. In most cases there is a dual-language text. This coffee-table book is a showcase of the work of award-winning artists many of whom were past winners of the prestigious *Hans Christian Andersen Award*. At the end of the book there is biographical information about the artists who have contributed to this volume: Janal Amambing (Malaysia), Muhammed Amous (Palestine), Mitsumasa Anno (Japan), Rotraut Susanne Berner (Germany), Pulak Biswas (India), Ora Eitan (Israel), Noemí Villamuza (Spain) and many others share their vision with other illustrators who are more familiar to the British audience such as Quentin Blake, Anthony Browne, Rosemary Wells and Lisbeth Zwerger just to mention a few. An amazing book that proves the fact that illustration in children's books is an art that is rapidly progressing throughout the world and acquiring the high status and respect that it deserves. IBBY (International Board on Books for Young People) will receive 15% of every book sold.

Thura's Diary: A Young Girl's Life in War-torn Baghdad

Thura Al-Windawi

Translated from Arabic by Robin Bray
Puffin Books (2004) PB £5.99 ISBN: 0 14 131769 8

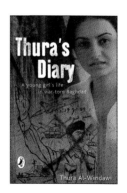

On 15th March 2003, a few days before the invasion of Iraq began, 19-year-old Thura, the eldest of three sisters from a close-knit, middle-class Shia Muslim family, began writing a diary. As the bombs fell on Baghdad her family were constantly on the move until they finally fled to the countryside. For two months Thura recorded her thoughts about the war, using it as a way of coming to terms with the chaos that surrounded her. The diary gives us a compelling insight into the way in which the war affected Thura, her family and friends, and how she dealt with the horror of war. Although she writes of her fears for the future of her country, she continues to hope for peace. The lives of many were and still are being destroyed in Iraq, but thankfully Thura's words, translated from the Arabic, survive and provide us with an eye-witness account.

How to Talk to Children About Art
Françoise Barbe-Gall

Translated from French by Phoebe Dunn
Frances Lincoln (2005) PB £9.99 ISBN: 0 7112 2388 2

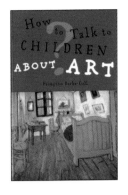

Aimed at adults rather than children, this will be an invaluable resource for teachers and parents who struggle to answer questions from the inquisitive mind of young children on the subject of art. It assumes no previous artistic or historical knowledge and it is not an art textbook. There are three main sections: the first part prepares you for a visit to a museum or art gallery and it has short but useful tips on what are the main problems and the areas that may interest children; the second section looks at different types of painting and covers techniques, portraits, landscapes, religious paintings and others; the third and last section examines 30 different types of paintings by great artists from fifteenth century religious artwork to twentieth century abstracts. Each picture has the basic information of title, date, painter and technique used as well as an examination of single details, a wide range of possible questions and their respective answers and an analysis of the work against its socio-historical background. This is a wonderful and unique resource that will help children to appreciate paintings and to look at them in a totally different way, but will also be an invaluable tool for all those eager to promote art amongst children and adults alike. Simple language, concise text and short paragraphs make this book easy to read and understand.

This is only a small selection of dual-language books and you will find many more titles available from b small publishing, Mantra Lingua and Milet Publishing. Frances Lincoln have also launched a new dual-language series.

What am I?
Aurélie Lanchais and Alain Crozon

Translated from French by Sarah Adams
Milet Publishing (2000) HB £5.99
ISBN: 1 84059 242 7

Who am I?
Aurélie Lanchais and Alain Crozon

Translated from French by Sarah Adams
Milet Publishing (2000) HB £5.99
ISBN: 1 84059 228 1

I can fly, what am I?
Alain Crozon

Translated from French by Sarah Adams
Milet Publishing (2000) HB £5.99
ISBN: 1 84059 249 4

I have wheels, what am I?
Alain Crozon

Translated from French by Sarah Adams
Milet Publishing (2000) HB £5.99
ISBN: 1 84059 235 4

These four books form part of a very original lift-the-flap series of interactive rhyme and riddle books. Each book consists of 21 fun riddles for children to solve together with brightly coloured artwork and lift-the-flaps that contain the answers to the riddles. *What am I?* helps children to identify different objects with the answer hidden behind the flaps, *Who am I?* identifies different animals, *I can fly, what am I?* identifies different things that can fly and *I have wheels, what am I?* identifies different things on wheels. The vibrancy of the colours and interaction of the flaps will absorb any young child. All four titles are available in an English single-language version. *What am I?* and *I can fly what am I?* are available in Arabic, Bengali, Chinese, French, Turkish and Urdu and *Who am I?* and *I have wheels, what am I?* are available in Chinese, French, Gujarati, Russian, Turkish and Vietnamese.

George's Garden ('Senses' Series)
Mandy and Ness

English/Bengali bilingual text
Translated into Bengali by Kanai Datta
Miliet Publishing (2000) PB £5.99
ISBN: 1 840 59164 1

Have lots of fun lifting the flaps and guessing what is hidden behind them, in this highly interactive picture book for the very young. George plays in the garden, building a sandcastle, planting his seeds, hiding behind a tree, playing football, and he also finds an insect and a flower! A picture book about touch which

teaches children about senses in a very enjoyable and friendly way. Each double spread has a short text in Bengali and English inviting the reader to speculate about the object hidden on the other half page containing the illustration and the lift-the-flap mechanism. There is a bold type face for each word representing each sense such as 'hard', 'rough', 'smooth' etc. which correlate to the object hidden behind the flap. This is an ideal book for reading aloud and for story time sessions as it encourages child participation. There are other titles in the series not to be missed – *Hattie's House*, *Peter's Party* and *Rosie's Room*.

Chameleon Swims
Laura Hambleton

English/Italian bilingual text
Translated into Italian by Roberta Umicini
Milet Publishing (2005) HB £5.99
ISBN: 1 84059 440 3

Chameleon Races
Laura Hambleton

English/Turkish bilingual text
Translated into Turkish by Dr Fatih Erdoğan
Milet Publishing (2005) HB £5.99
ISBN: 1 84059 432 2

Featuring characters from her popular book, *Welcome to Lizard Lounge* Chameleon, Gecko, Gila Monster and Salamander – the new Chameleon board book series by Laura Hambleton is now published simultaneously in English and 12 bilingual versions which provide parallel texts in various European, Asian and African languages. The non-English words are printed in bolder type and precede the English text, a strategy which foregrounds the first language, and would also reinforce to native English speakers that English is not everyone's first language, nor is it any more important than any other. Quite apart from their attraction for young readers, these books would be of great benefit to non-English-speaking adults reading to children. With incredibly bright, simple but subtle pictures, each double spread on a bold background, these are exciting, funny and cheerful little books, with simple but imaginative text, with well suited alliteration, assonance and onomatopoeia in the English text.

Lucy Cat at the Farm
Catherine Bruzzone, illustrated by Clare Beaton

French/English bilingual picture strip
Translated into French by
Marie-Thérèse Bougard
b small publishing (2005) PB £ 4.99
ISBN: 1 902915 11 9

Lucy Cat in Town
Catherine Bruzzone, illustrated by Clare Beaton

Spanish/English bilingual picture strip
Translated into Spanish by
Rosa Maria Martin
b small publishing (2005) PB £4.99
ISBN: 0 7641 3149 4

Two adventures of Lucy the Cat, both available in French and Spanish bilingual picture strip books. Somehow even the most ordinary trips turn into adventures for Lucy. When she visits the farm, she saves everyone from an escaping bull, while on a shopping trip in town with mum, brave Lucy stops a thief who tries to rob the supermarket. Delightful short stories with numbered picture strips to guide young readers through feature bold and colourful cartoon representations of Lucy and her animal friends and relatives. The carefully controlled bilingual text and frequent repetition will introduce young children to a foreign language in a natural, relaxed way. The language used in these books is fairly simple and so would be suitable for early readers and/or adults with little previous knowledge of the language wanting to read with children. A useful and simple-to-use pronunciation guide to identify new key words in the foreign language is included, together with a short, attractive key-word bilingual picture dictionary.

I'm Too Big

Lone Morton,
illustrated by Steve Weatherill

English/Spanish bilingual text
Translated into Spanish by Rosa Maria Martin
b small Publishing (1994) HB £5.99
ISBN: 0 8120 6451 8

I Want my Banana!

Mary Risk, illustrated
by Alex de Wolf

English/French bilingual text
Translated into French by Jacqueline Jansen
b small Publishing (1996) HB £5.99
ISBN: 1 874735 03 4

Here are two books to help young children learn a foreign language in a fun and engaging way. In *I'm Too Big*, Elephant and Giraffe are unhappy with the way they look. They want to be different – one would like to be taller, the other would like to be shorter, one would like to be yellow, the other grey. Finally, though, they agree that they are happy as they are! *I Want my Banana* finds little Monkey very upset. He's hungry and can't find his banana. The other jungle animals try to be helpful by offering him their own fruit but are they really being friendly? The 'I can read' series of language learning story books are delightful, appealing stories with bright, colourful artwork by well-known illustrators and easy-to-read bilingual text. They include helpful notes for parents and teachers, a picture dictionary with key words and a simplified guide to pronunciation. Ideal to use as an introduction to a foreign language.

Milet Picture Dictionary

Sedat Turhan,
illustrated by Sally Hagin

Milet Publishing (2003) HB £9.99
ISBN: 1 84059 354 7

Milet Mini Picture Dictionary

Sedat Turhan,
illustrated by Sally Hagin

Milet Publishing (2003) HB £5.99
ISBN: 1 84059 372 5

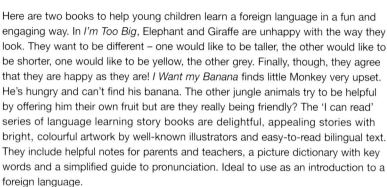

Flashwords

Sedat Turhan,
illustrated by Sally Hagin

Milet Publishing (2004) Box £5.99
ISBN: 184059 419 5

These two bilingual dictionaries and the flashwords are vibrant and original. They feature beautiful, colourful artwork that will allow the reader's creativity to be stimulated while they learn the words. In the *Milet Picture Dictionary* the objects are clearly identified, in their contexts or separately and key subjects are covered,

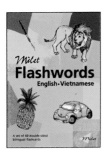

including: home, school, food, colours, plants, animals, clothing, communication and many others. The dictionary is available in English and also in 18 bilingual editions. The *Milet Mini Picture Dictionary* is in a smaller board book format containing many of the same key subjects. *Flashwords* is another innovative way to help children to learn another language. It is a set of 60 bilingual flash-cards featuring popular images from both the *Milet Picture Dictionary* and *Milet Mini Picture Dictionary* series. In the dual-language version, one side of the card features an object in colour with its word in English and, on the reverse side, the same image appears in black and white with its word in Turkish. An English only version is also available.

What is Peace?
Emma Damon

English/Portugese bilingual text
Mantra Lingua (2005) HB £8.50 ISBN: 1 84444 738 3

How do you explain peace to young children? Peace can be many things and this delightful and timely dual-language lift-the-flap book introduces the concepts of peace to the very young. It gives different examples on every page – peace is giving – not taking; listening – not arguing; friendship – not hate. It combines gentle texts with colourful illustrations by Emma Damon and there is a bright, colourful Peace Poster full of useful facts that can be put on the classroom wall. This book is available in 19 dual-language editions and in British Sign Language.

My Daddy is a Giant
Carl Norac, illustrated by Ingrid Godon

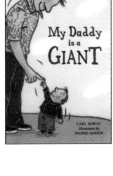

English/Italian bilingual text
Translated into Italian by Paola Antonioni
Mantra Lingua (2004) PB £7.50 ISBN: 1 84444 363 9

In his imagination a little boy sees his daddy as a giant – his dad is so tall that the clouds sleep over his shoulders, he sneezes like a hurricane, makes the ground shake when he runs and when he wants to cuddle him, he has to climb a ladder. Being a gentle giant, he loves his son with all his giant heart. This charming story reveals a very positive and comforting feeling – dad is not a scary giant after all, and where the boy feels safest is in his dad's arms. It focuses on the bond of love that link a father and a son. Carl Norac's lyrical text expresses the warmth of the father son relationship and is complemented by Ingrid Godon's rich, soft pastel tone illustrations.

Grandma Nana
Véronique Tadjo

English/Bengali bilingual text
Translated into Bengali by Kanai Datta
Milet Publishing (2000) PB £5.99 ISBN: 1 84059 287 7

Grandma Nana loves all children and she likes to laugh with them, tell them beautiful stories and pose riddles. Grandma Nana is a very wise woman and knows many important things from family history to all the plants that can be used to cure the sick. But Grandma Nana has something very special, a lucky charm doll, different from any other doll, that she keeps very close to her heart. This is a touching story that emphasises the important role that all grandmothers play in every culture. A dual-language picture book with text in English and Bengali. Véronique Tadjo's illustrations are a wonderful mix of black and white photographs and stunning artwork.

The Lucky Grain of Corn
Véronique Tadjo

English/Turkish bilingual text
Translated into Turkish by Dr Fatih Erdoḡan
Milet Publishing (2000) PB £5.99 ISBN: 1 84059 282 6

Soro's parents give him a lucky grain of corn, but when he leaves it on a stone the grain is stolen by a guinea-fowl who eats it. Soro runs after the bird from village to village and along the way he meets welcoming animals and people that invite him to stay with them. However, Soro cannot stay because he wants to recover his grain of corn. A magical tale with a surprise ending, told in rhythmic text accompanied by lively and colourful illustrations. The story, inspired by African traditions and folklore, will help children learn about different cultures. A dual-language picture book with text in English and Turkish.

Mamy Wata and the Monster
Véronique Tadjo

English/Somali bilingual text
Translated into Somali by Sulaiman Egeh
Milet Publishing (2000) PB £5.99 ISBN: 1 84059 270 2

Mamy Wata, the queen of all the waters, has a peaceful and happy life in her kingdom, swimming and playing in the waterfalls. But one day she hears that a horrible carnivorous monster has been frightening the people living in the surrounding villages. Determined to help, she decides to hide in the monster's cave and wait for him. When the monster arrives he bursts into tears and because Mamy Wata is so deeply touched she decides to make him happy again. A dual-language picture book, with text in English and Somali and vivid and rich illustrations by Véronique Tadjo. This wonderful folk tale would be enjoyable for reading aloud as well as independent reading.

The Little Red Hen and the Grains of Wheat
L. R. Hen, illustrated by Jago

English/Croatian bilingual text
Translated into Croatian by Dubravka Janekovic
Mantra Lingua (2005) PB £7.50 ISBN: 1 84444 203 9

One day Little Red Hen finds some grains of wheat when walking through the farmyard, but when she asks the cat, the dog and the goose for help to plant them, no one is willing to help her. When the wheat grows and is ripe she asks for help to harvest it, then to thresh it, to grind it into flour and finally to bake it into bread. But every time she asks for help everyone is always too busy! However, when Little Red Hen has turned the wheat into freshly baked bread, suddenly all the other farmyard animals are willing to help her eat it. This is a delightful retelling of a classic fable. With the simplicity of its text and gentle repetition it will encourage children to take an active role and participate in reading the story aloud. Children will enjoy the humour of the character drawings and a valuable lesson about the importance of teamwork.

Ali Baba and the Forty Thieves
Enebor Attard, illustrated by Richard Holland

English/Kurdish bilingual text
Translated into Kurdish by Anwar Soltani
Mantra Lingua (2005) PB £7.50 ISBN: 1 84444 413 9

On the night of a full moon Ali Baba discovers a dark cave where a gang of thieves are hiding their treasure and the revelation of this secret leads his greedy brother Cassim to his death. When Ali Baba recovers the body of his brother, the thieves realise that someone else knows the secret of the cave so they decide to kill him. Ali Baba's clever slave Morgianna outwits the thieves and avenges Cassim's death by killing the villains. Enebor Attard's retelling of one of the all time favourite classic stories from the tales of the Arabian Nights is deftly done. The tale encapsulates the moral lesson where honesty and cleverness succeed and greed is punished. The wonderful collage artwork with rich colours and beautiful scenes recreates the magical essence of the traditional Arabian tales.

Journey Through Islamic Art
Na'ima bint Robert, illustrated by Diana Mayo

English/Bengali bilingual text
Translated into Bengali by Sujata Banerjee
Mantra Lingua (2005) HB £8.50 ISBN: 1 84444 334 5

A young girl follows the silken thread of her imagination as it takes flight and carries her on a wonderful and magical journey. From great mosques and ancient cities to ornamental gardens, she travels through the rich and artistic heritage of Islamic civilization. The lyrical text by Na'ima bint Robert is complemented by Diana Mayo's stunning illustrations that bring all the tremendous beauty of Islamic art to life. This book is available in 22 dual-language editions and is ideal for use in the classroom. At the back of the book there is a useful page of explanations of the ancient monuments and artefacts, places and sacred texts mentioned in the text. Na'ima bint Robert has also written *The Swirling Hijaab*, illustrated by Nilesh Mistry, also available from Mantra.

Chanda and the Mirror of Moonlight
Margaret Bateson Hill, illustrated by Karin Littlewood

English/Hindi bilingual text
Translated into Hindi by Asha Kathoria
Zero to Ten (2003) PB £4.99 ISBN: 1 84089 305 2

Set in Rajasthan, India, this story draws on themes from traditional folktales. Chanda's life is completely changed when her mother dies and her father remarries. Her stepmother and stepsister are cruel and she is reduced to a life of servitude following the death of her father. She seeks solace walking by the river and sitting in the shade of the old banyan tree while she gazes into the magic mirror that her mother left to her. One day she meets a handsome young man, falls in love, and despite despicable deception and plotting by her stepmother and stepsister she eventually finds true happiness. Similar to the 'Cinderella' story, this dual-language story is lavishly illustrated by watercolours that reflect the dazzling colours discovered by Karin Littlewood on her visits to India. A supplementary section at the back of the book explains the mirror work incorporated in many Indian textiles together with information about the Hindi language.

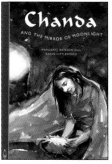

A Summer Full of Love
Füruzan

English/Turkish bilingual text
Translated from Turkish by Damian Croft
Milet Publishing (2001) PB £5.99
ISBN: 1 84059 301 4

A Cup of Turkish Coffee
Buket Uzuner

English/Turkish bilingual text
Translated from Turkish by Pelin Arıner
Milet Publishing (2001) PB £5.99
ISBN: 1 84059 300 8

Radical Niyazi Bey
Muzaffer Izgü

English/Turkish bilingual text
Translated from the Turkish by Damian Croft
Milet Publishing (2001) PB £5.99
ISBN: 1 84059 299 0

There are five books in this series of short story dual-language books in English and Turkish. *A Summer Full of Love* is a collection of eloquent stories in parallel Turkish-English text for older adolescents. Füruzan is noted for her sensitive characterisations, often of the poor, and of women and children. The

writing style of these three stories reflects both the culture and philosophy of Turkey, and presents quite a challenge for readers unused to a poetic, picaresque tradition. This is a book of great seriousness, which simultaneously disturbs, intrigues and poses questions. It offers an insight into a totally different way of viewing life, and raises many debates concerning culture and expectations. The parallel texts would assist Turkish speaking learners of English, whilst fascinating those who have no Turkish. A challenging and immensely rewarding read.

In *A Cup of Turkish Coffee* a recipe for authentic Turkish coffee serves as an introduction to a collection of four evocative short stories. Through these unusual narratives, Buket Uzuner transports the reader on a journey in which apparently trivial anecdotes give a deep insight into the psychology of the characters, their dreams, their thoughts and their sense of belonging. The book, aimed at both teenagers and adults, is published in parallel Turkish-English text. It gives a good insight into the work of one of the most celebrated authors in contemporary Turkish Literature for readers of both languages.

Radical Niyazi Bey by Muzaffer Izgü, introduces various aspects of Turkish life – family, social and political – that illustrate the different traditions and customs with a deft and perceptive humour that will appeal to readers of both languages. This book consists of five independent stories with parallel texts in English and Turkish.

The final two books in the series: *Fourth Company* by Rifat Ilgaz contains warm and witty stories about the travails of life in military service, holidays at home and the pathological fear of doctors, and in *Out of the Way! Socialism's Coming!* Aziz Nesin turns his uniquely incisive, satirical wit on shifting ideologies, bureaucracy and the question of who's really (in)sane!

Other titles available

The famous Frog books by Max Velthuijs (some of which are reviewed on page 36) are produced in dual-language editions by Milet. *Frog and the Wide World* and *Frog is a Hero* are available in Bengali, Chinese, Gujarati, Punjabi, Turkish, Urdu and Vietnamese. *Frog and the Stranger* and *Frog is Frog* are available in Albanian, Bengali, Chinese, Somali, Turkish, Urdu and Vietnamese.

The popular Lars the Polar Bear series by Hans de Beer are available in dual-language from North-South Books. *Little Polar Bear and the Husky Pup* is available in French and German, *Little Polar Bear Take Me Home!* is available in German and *Little Polar Bear* is available in French.

Frances Lincoln have reissued three of their most enduring multi-cultural picture books in dual-language format. The books will be available in Gujarati, Punjabi, Bengali and Urdu, with parallel English text: *Amazing Grace* by Mary Hoffman, and two Jessica Souhami titles *The Leopard's Drum* and *Rama and the Demon King*.

Contributors

Philip Pullman was born in 1946 in Norwich, England and grew up in Zimbabwe and Wales. He won the New English Library first novel competition a year after graduating. He worked as a teacher for many years and his first children's novel *The Ruby in the Smoke*, the first of a quartet of Victorian thrillers, was published in 1992. He has won many awards for his children's books, including the *Carnegie Medal*, the *Guardian Award*, the *Smarties Prize*, the *Whitbread Book of the Year Award* for *The Amber Spyglass*, part of his acclaimed fantasy trilogy, *His Dark Materials*, and the prestigious *Astrid Lindgren Memorial Award* in 2005. Philip lives in Oxford with his wife and two children, one a professional musician and the other studying at Cambridge.

Nicholas Tucker is honorary Senior Lecturer in Cultural Studies at the University of Sussex. A former teacher and then an educational psychologist, he is the author of nine books about children, childhood and reading, including *The Child and the Book*. He has also written six books for children, broadcasts frequently and reviews in the *Independent* and for all three *Times* supplements. Recent publications include *Family Fictions: Contemporary Classics of Children's Literature*, *The Rough Guide to Children's Books*, *The Rough Guide to Teenage Books* and *Darkness Visible: Inside the World of Philip Pullman*.

Sarah Adams was born in 1970 in Brussels, Belgium. She has worked as an arts critic and travel journalist and critic reporting on cultural melting pots from Harlem to Marseille, and her writing has appeared regularly in national newspapers and on bbc.co.uk/arts. Sarah has translated three works by Daniel Pennac; *Dog*, *Kamo's Escape* and *Eye of the Wolf* which won the 2005 *Marsh Award for Children's Literature in Translation* and was chosen for the 2004 IBBY Honour List. Sarah has also translated other children's books including *The Boy Who Ate Stars* by Kochka, the 'Golem' series by Marie-Aude, Lorris and Elvire Murail, the *Who Am I?* picture book series and *Super H* for Milet Publishing. Sarah is London-based and has also lived and worked in Greece and Argentina.

Lene Kaaberbol was born in Copenhagen and published her first book at the age of fifteen. She is a graduate of Aarhus University, and has taught English and Drama to high school students in Copenhagen. Lene has published many books in Denmark, several of which have been translated into other languages. In May 2002, she won the Disney Writer of the Year Award for her work on the W.I.T.C.H. series of books. *The Shamer's Daughter*, which was translated from the Danish by the author herself, was shortlisted for the 2005 *Marsh Award for Children's Literature in Translation*.

Gillian Lathey is Reader in Children's Literature at Roehampton University and Acting Director of the National Centre for Research in Children's Literature. She was for many years an infant teacher in north London, and combines interests in children, childhood and literature by teaching an MA in Children's Literature, supervising doctoral students in Children's Literature, and researching the practices and history of translating for children. She also administers the biennial *Marsh Award for Children's Literature in Translation*.

Patricia Billings is Director of Milet Publishing, a leading publisher of bilingual children's books, with over 350 bilingual editions in English with 25 languages, including Albanian, Arabic, Bengali, Chinese, Kurdish, Somali, Turkish, Urdu, Vietnamese and so on. Milet also publishes a line of artistic children's books in English, thirteen of which were translated from other languages, such as French, German and Turkish. Before founding Milet with her partner Sedat Turhan in 1995, Patricia worked as a journalist, editor and researcher on Middle East and human rights issues, based in Washington, DC and in the Middle East. Her academic background includes a degree in Political Science and Middle East Politics and post-graduate work in Arab Studies and Film Studies.

Klaus Flugge was born in Germany in 1934. He trained as a bookseller in Leipzig but his political views forced him to flee East Germany in 1953. He arrived in New York in 1957 and worked for Abelard-Schuman who, in 1961, asked him to run their London office. He became Managing Director and Publisher of adult and children's books and began originating his own books, which included titles by Edward Ardizzone, Joan Aiken and David McKee. In 1976, Klaus set up his own publishing company – Andersen Press – named in tribute to Hans Christian Andersen. Andersen Press specialises in picture books and children's fiction and now consists of over 900 published titles, the majority of which are still in print. Klaus received the *Eleanor Farjeon Award*, for outstanding contribution to children's books, in 1999.

Neal Hoskins founded WingedChariot Press in 2004. Previously he worked in educational publishing at Oxford University Press. He now sees picture books as a perfect conduit for European co-operation, understanding and enjoyment.

Authors & Illustrators

Beatrice Alemagna was born in 1973 in Bologna, Italy and studied Art at the Istituto Superiore for industrial arts in Urbino. She moved to France aged 23 and has worked as an illustrator and writer of children's picture books as well as producing collages and posters. She has won numerous awards for her illustration, including the *Futures's Figures* prize in Montreuil, and had the first exhibition of her work in 2003 in Charleville-Mézierès in France. Beatrice lives in Paris.

Thura Al-Windawi was born in Iraq and comes from a close-knit, middle-class Shia Muslim family. She started writing a diary at the age of 19 a few days before the start of the war in Iraq in 2003. She was offered a full financial-aid grant to attend the University of Pennsylvania in 2003.

Lena Anderson was born in 1939 in Sweden. She produced her best-selling book about Linnea in 1984 together with author, Christina Björk. She has produced several books about Linnea and many picture books. *Linnea in Monet's Garden* has sold over 700,000 copies in the USA and was awarded the foremost children's book prize in Germany in both 1984 and 1988. Lena and Christina Björk received the *Astrid Lindgren Prize* in 1998. She lives in Stockholm.

David B. was born Pierre-François Beauchard in a small town near Orléans, France and is a founding member of L'Association, a group of French cartoonists who banded together as publishers in 1990 and have revolutionised European comics with their groundbreaking approach to format, subject matter, and style. He has received many awards, including the French *Alph-Art* award for comics excellence in 2000, and he was cited as European Cartoonist of the Year in 1998 by *The Comics Journal*. David lives in France.

Françoise Barbe-Gall is a teacher of Art History at the Ecole du Louvre and lecturer for the cultural association 'Comment Regarder un Tableau' (CO.RE.TA). She has also taught at the New York University in Paris and the Censier University in Paris. She lives in Paris with her husband and three children.

Margaret Bateson Hill was born and grew up in Blackpool, Lancashire, England. She studied Drama and English at university, going on to run drama workshops for children. Margaret has written several books for children including *Lao Lao of Dragon Mountain*, *Shota and the Starquilt* and *Masha and the Firebird*, which won the English Association's award for the Best Illustration Picture Book of 1999. She now spends her time storytelling throughout the country and lives in Brixton, London.

Jutta Bauer was born in 1955 in Germany. She is one of the best-known picture book illustrators and cartoonists in Europe. Jutta has published numerous picture and children's books and received awards, including the *German Youth Literature Prize*. Jutta lives in Hamburg.

Klaus Baumgart lives in Berlin, Germany. He is the author and illustrator of the *Laura's Star* series. These books have become international best-sellers and a feature film of *Laura's Star* has been made. Klaus was the first German author/illustrator to be shortlisted for *The Children's Book Award* in 1999 for *Laura's Star*.

Clare Beaton graduated from Hornsey College of Art, London, with first-class honours and then worked for eight years at the BBC, illustrating for various children's programmes. She now works as a freelance illustrator and writer of children's books. Clare lives in London with her partner and three children.

Gunilla Bergström was born in 1942 in Sweden. An enormously prolific writer and illustrator, she is regarded as one of the most successful picture book creators in Sweden where her Alfie Atkins books have won the hearts of generations of young Swedish readers as well as gaining a wide international readership. In 2002 Alfie celebrated 30 years and the occasion was marked by the publication of two new picture books *How far can Alfie Reach?* and *Alfie's ABC*. Gunilla has won numerous awards since her debut in 1972, including the *Elsa Beskow Plaque* in 1979 and the *Astrid Lindgren Prize* in 1981.

Pablo Bernasconi (see page 27)

Rotraut Susanne Berner was born in 1948 in Stuttgart, Germany. She studied graphic design at the College of Graphic Design in Munich, then spent several years in advertising before becoming an independent graphic artist and illustrator in 1977. In 1983 she won the *Celestino Piatti Prize*, the first of about 15 awards.

Pulak Biswas is one of the most senior children's book illustrators in India. Based in Delhi, he began his art career more than forty years ago, working for several advertising agencies before becoming a freelance artist in 1981. He now concentrates on painting and children's book illustration. Pulak has worked for a number of publishers in India and overseas. Among other awards, his book *Tiger on a Tree* won a plaque at the *Biennial of Illustrations Bratislava*.

Christina Björk was born in 1938 in Sweden. She is a journalist and author of several extremely successful books together with the illustrator, Lena Anderson. In 1988 she and Lena received the *Astrid Lindgren Prize*. Christina lives in Stockholm.

Alison Boyle is an author, editor and consultant. She has a degree in English and Design as well as a Postgraduate Diploma in Publishing. She has written several children's books and also runs literacy workshops in schools and libraries.

Thomas Brezina is a successful author of adventure and detective books for children and teenagers, a television presenter for Austrian Television and is also involved in the production of school textbooks and videos about famous composers. He has also written a series of non-fiction books called 'Museum of Adventures'. His stories have been filmed for cinema and television, adapted as musicals, stage and radio plays and turned into interactive CD-ROM games. Thomas has received numerous prizes and awards for his work including the Golden Achievement Honour of the Austrian Republic. He has been an official ambassador for UNICEF since 1996 and lives in Vienna.

Dick Bruna was born in 1927 in Utrecht, the Netherlands. He grew up in Zeist and developed a keen interest in art and drawing during his school years. His father became one of the Netherlands' largest publishers, A.W. Bruna & Zoom and over the years Dick worked on the graphic design of books published by the company. He designed over 2,000 book jackets but it was in 1955 that his best-known creation, Miffy, the little rabbit, appeared. By 1975, the Miffy series had taken off and Dick was well established as a children's author and illustrator. Miffy has just celebrated 50 years.

Catherine Bruzzone taught Italian and French in secondary schools before joining Harrap as a junior editor of foreign language learning books many years ago. She moved to Pan Books to develop among others the *Breakthrough Language* series and then started her own business, b small publishing, in 1990. b small specialises in bilingual books for very young language learners: first words, stories and activity books. Catherine has two (bilingual) daughters and lives on Eel Pie Island in Twickenham, England.

Flavia Bujor was born in Romania and moved to France with her parents when she was two years old. She started writing her first novel *The Prophecy of the Gem* when she was 13. Since its publication in 2002 in France it has been translated into 23 languages. She is now working on her second novel.

Marianne Busser was born in the Netherlands. She writes articles for newspapers and magazines and with her partner, Ron Schröder, children's stories and songs for magazines, radio programmes and television shows. They live in the Netherlands with their three daughters, Anne, Jette and Liselotje.

Stefan Casta was born in 1949 in Vadstena, Sweden. He has been a journalist and naturalist and has made several natural history films. Stefan has won several awards including the *August Prize* and the *Nils Holgersson Plaque* in 2000 and the prestigious *Astrid Lindgren* prize in 2002 for his break through book, *Spelar Dod* (*Play Dead*). Several of his books have been translated into German and his first book to be translated into English is *Summer with Mary-Lou*.

David Chotjewitz was born in 1964 in Berlin, Germany. He is a teacher and a play-wright. He wrote his first book in 1984 and since then has written radio plays and a novel on Albert Einstein, *The Adventure of Thinking*. He lives in Hamburg with his daughter.

Alan Clarke was born in 1976 in Dublin, Ireland. He studied architecture at the Dublin Institute of Technology and then illustration at Falmouth College of Arts in Cornwall. Since graduating he has earned his living as a freelance illustrator, sculptor and designer.

Peter Cohen was born in 1946 in Sweden. He is a director, film producer and author.

Together with Olof Landström he has created films and books for children that have received international prizes. He has lived both in Germany and in Sweden and is now living in Stockholm.

Sandra Comino was born in Argentina. She is a writer of novels and short stories, is a teacher and an active member of ALIJA (the Argentine section of the International Board on Books for Young People) and organises writing and reading workshops training teachers and librarians throughout Argentina. She also works as a journalist and literary critic. Sandra won the *A La Orilla del Viento Prize* in 1999 and the *Para Leer el XXI Prize* in 2001.

Philippe Corentin was born in 1936 in Paris, France. He has been publishing cartoons since the late 1960s and is renowned in France for his popular and humorous children's picture books. He lives in Normandy.

Christopher Corr was born in London and studied at the Royal College of Art. His round the world travels provided much inspiration for his work and his first trip to India in 1986 resulted in a one person show entitled 'Welcome To India' which was followed by a book and a short BBC TV film of the same name. Commissions include book jackets, posters, the World Aids Day 1996 campaign, artist for Qantas, artist for Windstar Cruises and children's books.

Alain Crozon was born in Paris and studied graphic design at art schools there. He works as an art teacher and designs for magazines, as well as creating children's books. He co-authored the *Who am I? What am I?* series with Aurélie Lanchais.

Francisco Cunha was born in 1970 in Vila Do Conde, Portugal. He always had a passion for cartoons and studied at the Saint-Luc Art Institute in Liège, Belgium in 1999. He discovered the wonderful world of children's literature and *My Very Own Lighthouse* is his first picture book.

Francesco D'Adamo is well-known for his adult books in the tradition of Italian noir fiction. He began writing fiction for young adults in 1999 to much critical acclaim. His third novel, *Iqbal*, has been translated into 10 languages and also appears as a schools edition with notes. He lives in Milan, Italy.

Hans de Beer was born in 1957 in Muiden, the Netherlands. He started drawing as a child and after studying history at college, he went on to do illustration at the Rietveld Academy of Art in Amsterdam. Hans has illustrated various children's series including his first picture book about *Lars, the Little Polar Bear*, which has been seen on BBC Television and was made into a film in 2003 by Warner Brothers. He lives in Amsterdam with his wife.

Els de Groen lives in Bennekom, a Dutch town not far from Arnhem. In the troubled last decade of the twentieth century she travelled widely in the Balkans and this experience became central to her novel *No Roof in Bosnia*. It was short-listed for the *Marsh Award for Children's Literature in Translation* and was the UK IBBY Honours choice for a novel in translation in 1998.

Philippe Derrien was born in 1971 in France. He studied in Visual Expression at the Dupéré School of Paris and decorative Arts in Strasbourg and has become a popular and celebrated creator of children's books in France. In addition to his children's books, he creates illustrations for magazines and advertising. *Super H* is his first children's book to be published in English. Philippe lives and works in Nice.

Alex de Wolf was born in 1958 in Amstelveen, a suburb of Amsterdam, the Netherlands. He

studied at art college, and because he liked drawing animals and children most of all, he often sat sketching at the zoo for hours. Alex's first book for Nord-Süd Verlag was published in 1994. He lives with his wife and two small sons in Amsterdam.

Olivier Douzou was born in 1963 in France. He was one of the founders of Editions du Rouergue and directed its youth section. He is an author and illustrator as well as working in communications, design and graphics.

Daniela Drescher was born in 1966 in Munich, Germany. After graduating she lived for a while in Switzerland and the USA. Daniela trained in art therapy and has worked with children for ten years and is an illustrator for a parenting magazine.

Jacques Duquennoy studied Fine Art at the University of Paris and went on to establish a writing and illustration workshop where he produced materials for use in schools. He also worked as a primary school teacher before his first picture book was published in 1994 by Albin Michel. He currently has 34 titles published in 12 different countries. Jacques lives in France.

Lilian Edvall lives in Stockholm, Sweden and is a freelance journalist and author of several children's books including *The Rabbit Who Didn't Want to Go to Sleep* and *The Rabbit Who Longed for Home*.

Hans Magnus Enzensberger was born in 1929 in Bavaria, Germany. He is one of Germany's most prolific writers of poetry, prose, drama and cultural criticism and one of Europe's leading political thinkers. Widely translated, his writings represent a major contribution to world literature. He has received numerous distinguished prizes for his poetry, children's books and essays, including the *Pasolini Prize*. His two children's books, *The Number Devil* and *Where were you Robert?* which won the *Marsh Award for Children's Literature in Translation* in 2003, have become international best-sellers. He lives and works in Munich.

Eva Eriksson was born in Halmstad, on the southwest coast of Sweden. She was educated at the art school Konstfack in Stockholm and her first picture book was published in 1978. Eva is one of Sweden's most beloved creators of children's books and has written and/or illustrated many books. In 1979 she started her successful collaboration with Barbro Lindgren. Eva was the recipient of the *Astrid Lindgren Award* in 2001. She lives with her family in Stockholm.

Inga-Karin Eriksson was born in 1956 in Sweden. She has worked as an engraver and since 1985 as a freelance illustrator.

Tiny Fisscher was born in 1958 in the Netherlands. After working in many different occupations she made her writing debut in 1999 with *En dan was ik de prinses* which was published in English as *The Princess Gift Book*. Tiny has written five other books and also works as a sports instructor. She lives with her partner, daughter and dog near the centre of Amsterdam.

Cornelia Funke was born in 1958 in Dorsten, Germany. She studied education theory at university in Hamburg and worked for three years on an educational project while completing a course in book illustration at the Hamburg State College of Design. After working as a designer for board games and illustrator of children's books, she became an author herself. Cornelia has written over 40 books and become an international best-selling children's author with her books being translated into many languages. *The Thief Lord* won the *Swiss Youth*

Literature Award and the *Zurich Children's Book Award* from the Vienna House of Literature. A feature film is being made of her novel *Inkheart*. Aside from her novels, Cornelia works for the German state television channel ZDF and lives in Hamburg with her husband and two children.

Füruzan was born in 1935 in Istanbul, Turkey. She is one of Turkey's most popular and critically acclaimed writers, most well known for her short stories. Her first book, *Paraziz Yatili* (1972), was awarded the *Sait Faik Prize*, Turkey's top prize for short stories, and her work has received numerous other awards. The film made from Füruzan's books, *Benim Sinemalarim*, was screened at the 1990 Cannes Film Festival. Her books have been translated into English, German, Russian, Dutch, Swedish, Arabic and Persian.

Andrew Fusek Peters is an Anglo-Czech poet, children's author, didgeridoo player, broadcaster, anthologist and creative writing tutor. He has worked in thousands of schools, libraries, art centres and literary festivals since 1987. His family fled Prague during the Russian coup of 1948 and this background has greatly influenced his many books, which include *The Barefoot Book of Strange and Spooky Stories*, *May the Angels be With Us* and *The Weather's Getting Worse*. Andrew has been a presenter and writer for BBC 1's *Wham Bam Strawberry Jam* and has done much work on Radio 4 and as a performer/writer in education. He lives in Shropshire, England.

Jostein Gaarder was born in 1952 in Oslo, Norway and is one of the most popular Scandinavian authors. He attended the University of Oslo where he studied Scandinavian languages and theology and began contributing to several textbooks on philosophy and theology. He was a teacher of philosophy before becoming an author in 1986. This was followed by two children's books, *The Solitaire Mystery*, published in 1990, which won both the *Norwegian Literary Critics' Award* and the *Ministry of Cultural and Scientific Affairs Literary Prize*, and his great international best-selling novel about philosophy, *Sophie's World* which appeared in 1991. It has now sold over 16 million copies in nearly 50 languages. In 1997 Jostein and his wife, Siri Dannevig, formed the Sofie Foundation to promote a sustainable environment. He lives in Oslo with his wife and two teenage sons.

Sally Gardner was a theatre designer and specialised in costume for 15 years before moving into children's books as a full-time illustrator and writer. She is the illustrator of *Hallo? Is Anybody There?* by Jostein Gaarder, *Tales from the Box* which is a series of books about a box of toys and their adventures and *Polly Running Away Book*. Sally was the winner of the 2003 *Nestlé Smarties Book Prize* Bronze Award for *The Countess's Calamity* in the 6-8 category. Her most recent book is *I Coriander*. Sally lives in North London with her three children.

Anna Gavalda was born in Eure-et-Loir in France. She was a French teacher for a number of years and worked as a journalist. She devoted herself to writing full-time after the success of her first book, an adult novel called *I Wish Someone Were Waiting for Me Somewhere*, which has sold over 700,000 copies in France and has been translated into over 30 languages. Her first children's novel was *35 Kilos of Hope*. Anna lives with her family in Seine-et-Marne, France.

Peter Geibler was born 1962 in Germany. He studied philosophy in Munich and went on to work as a journalist and editor. He writes poetry for adults and *Yours and Mine* is his first book for children. Peter lives with his wife and son.

Sarah Gibb studied at Ravensbourne and Central St. Martins Colleges, London and did an MA at Brighton, graduating in 1996. While still at art college, she designed a range of cards, *High Life* for Arts Angels that has grown to include notebooks, wrapping paper and calendars. Her book cover for *The Nanny Diaries* was reproduced as a poster on the Underground and she illustrated the covers for the eight books in the *Adrian Mole* series by Sue Townsend.

Sara Gimbergsson is an art director who has illustrated picture books published in Sweden including *The Rabbit Who Didn't Want to Go to Sleep*. She lives in Gothenburg with her husband and two children.

Amelie Glienke studied painting and visual communication in Berlin, Germany. Today she works as a freelance illustrator and cartoonist.

Angelika Glitz was born in 1966 in Hanover, Germany. She studied management economics and worked for some years in advertising. Angelika has written many books for children as well as for theatre, radio and television. She lives in Frankfurt with her husband and three children.

Ingrid Godon is a Belgian illustrator and her work has rapidly gained international acclaim. Her first picture book, *What Shall We Do With The Boo Hoo Baby?*, was hugely successful and translated into ten languages. *Hallo, Sailor* won several international awards including the *Golden Pencil* 2001 for the best picture book in the Netherlands. Ingrid lives in Belgium with her husband and three children.

Max Grafe is a printmaker, painter and illustrator. He has illustrated *Old Coyote* by Nancy Wood and the front cover of *Eye of the Wolf* by Daniel Pennac. He lives in New Orleans, USA.

David Grossman was born in 1954 in Jerusalem, Israel, and is recognised as one of the leading Israeli novelists of his generation. He studied philosophy and theatre at the Hebrew

University and began a 25-year career at Israel Radio at the age of ten as a correspondent for youth broadcasts. He has won many prizes in Israel, including *The Prime Minister Prize for Hebrew Literature* and *The Publishers' Association Prize for Best Novel in Hebrew*. His first book to be published in English, *The Yellow Wind*, described his journey into Palestinian camps on the West Bank and Gaza Strip in 1987. One of his acclaimed books *The ZigZag Kid* was winner of both the *Premio Grinzane* and *Premio Mondelo* in Italy.

Wilhelm Gruber was born in 1950 in a small town on the Ems river in Germany. He is a teacher of reading at a school for children with reading difficulties. *The Upside-down Reader*, his first book for children was published in 1998 and was Book of the Month at the Akademie für Kinder-und Jugendliteratur, Volkach. Wilhelm lives with his family in Münster.

Jaap ter Haar (1922-1998) was born in 1922 in the Netherlands. His studies were interrupted when the Germans entered Holland in 1940 and he became a member of the Underground Movement. He started writing stories for his own four children in 1949 and from then on he became a full-time writer. In addition to books, he wrote plays for radio and television. Jaap ter Haar's books have been translated into many languages and he received literary awards for his work in several countries.

Sally Hagin is an Honours graduate of the Norwich School of Art and is an arts teacher as well as an illustrator. She is the illustrator of Milet's most popular range of picture dictionaries, including the *The Milet Picture Dictionary, Milet Mini Picture Dictionary* and *Milet Flashwords*.

Laura Hambleton is an Honours graduate of the Norwich School of Art and Design. She is a successful designer and presents her books and gives workshops at festivals, bookstores, schools and activity centres throughout Britain. Laura is the creator of *I'm Afraid Too*, Commended Winner of the 2002 *V&A Illustration Awards*, illustrator of the popular *How Bees Be*, and creator of the highly praised *Welcome to Lizard Lounge*, *Chameleon Races* and *Chameleon Swims*.

Wolfram Hänel was born in 1956 in Fulda, Germany, but soon moved to Hanover, where he studied German and English language and literature, worked as a theatre photographer, commercial artist, advertising copywriter, probationary teacher and theatre director. In 1991 he won the playwrights's prize awarded by the league of German theatres. Wolfram writes plays, children's books and travel guides. He received the *Kurt Marwietz Literature Prize* from the city of Hanover for his work as a whole in 2001. Wolfram lives with his family in Hanover and in West Cork, Ireland.

Vanessa Hié was born in 1974 In France. Ever since she learnt how to hold a pen, she has been drawing and went on to study the arts. She has illustrated several children's books and also manufactures small toy animals from papier mâché. *Those Messy Hempels* is her first picture book. Vanessa lives in Paris with her husband and son.

Anne Holm (1922-1998) was born in 1922 in Denmark. She trained as a journalist and her first book was published in 1956. This was followed by two more titles in Danish before *I am David* was published in 1963 and translated into English in the same year. The novel has been in continuous print since then and is regarded as a modern classic. *I am David* has been televised, radio broadcast and translated in 16 countries on four continents. Anne was a member of the Danish Authors Society and travelled extensively throughout Europe. Her books won numerous awards including the Prize for Best Scandinavian Children's Book in 1963.

Biographies

Philip Hopman has collaborated on many children's picture books with Tjibbe Velskamp. *22 Orphans* was awarded a Silver Brush, an important Dutch award, in 1999. Philip created the line drawings for *The Frog Castle* by Jostein Gaarder.

Isabel Hoving was born in the Netherlands and lectures in comparative literature at the University of Leiden in Holland, specialising in post-colonial writing and issues of immigration. She spent a lot of time in Senegal, West Africa where she was invited to join a group of anthropologists to research oral traditions. Many of the multi-cultural references in *The Dream Merchant* are influenced by her study of Africa and her time there. *The Dream Merchant* is her first novel. It was awarded the *Golden Kiss Award* in 2003, the highest accolade for children's books in the Netherlands. Isabel lives in Amsterdam with her husband and teenage son.

E.T.W. Igel was born in 1960 in Hamburg, Germany. After school he began his training in business but soon stopped to attend the College for Graphics and Design. In 1987 he finished his further education by studying German and history. Today he is a freelance author and lives in Hamburg.

Muzaffer Izgü was born in 1933 in Adana, Turkey. He is one of Turkey's most popular and prolific writers, having written over 90 books for adults and children, including the ever-popular *Bando Takimi*, as well as theatre plays and screenplays. His work has won numerous prizes and his stories depict the realities of life in Turkey with sharp yet affectionate humour. Muzaffer was a teacher for decades and is respected as much for his excellence in this profession as for his writing.

Amélie Jackowski was born in 1976 in Toulon, France. She studied illustration at Strasbourg School of Decorative Arts and then went on to study at Aix-en-Provence University. Amélie's work has been exhibited at the Bologna Children's Book Fair in 1999, 2000, 2001 and at La Conciergerie in Paris, 2002. Amélie lives in Marseille close to the harbour.

Jean-Pierre Jâggi was born in 1954 in Zurich, Switzerland. He worked as a radio electrician and as a taxi, lorry and bus driver. In 1989 he moved to La Chaux-de-Fonds and worked as a bicycle designer and Shiatsu therapist. Fairy tales and fantasy stories have always played an important role in Jean-Pierre's life and when he was a courier he would tell his group stories which were frequently taken from actual incidents and embroidered to make great stories.

Jago is a nationally published, award-winning, extremely modest illustrator of the finest children's picture books. He lives in Cornwall with his wife.

Yvonne Jagtenberg is an artist based in Holland. *First Day at School* is her first book published in English.

Hervé Jubert was born in 1970, in Rheims, France. After finishing school he moved to Paris, where amongst other things he made video games, was a chauffeur, a butcher, and a drummer for a garage-punk-rock band. After studying art history he decided to go for an option he had been considering since he was five years old and he became an author. *Dance of the Assassins* was his first novel, followed by *Devil's Tango*. Hervé now lives with his wife and child in the southwest of France.

Reinhardt Jung (1949-1999) was born in 1949 in Germany. After graduating, he worked as a journalist and advertising copywriter in Berlin. From 1974, he worked with an international children's organisation and then went on to work in children's broadcasting in Stuttgart in 1992.

He wrote *Dreaming in Black and White* in 1996 and *Bambert's Book of Missing Stories* in 1998.

Lene Kaaberbol (see page 14 and 93)

Jakob Kirchmayr was born 1975 in
Innsbruck, Austria. For four years he studied painting in Innsbruck followed by further studies of restoration and conservation at the Academy for Applied Arts in Vienna. He then concentrated wholly on illustrating children's books. In 2000 he gained a scholarship for children's book illustrators in the City of Vienna where he lives.

Kochka was born in the Lebanon in 1964 of a
French father and a Lebanese mother. As a result of the war in 1976, the family went into exile in France. She studied law and qualified, but in 1997 decided to abandon the legal profession and devote herself to writing. Kochka is a recognised author in France of over 20 titles aimed at readers from three to young adult.

Almud Kunert was born in Bayreuth in
Germany. She studied painting and graphic design in Munich where she works as a freelance illustrator. She has illustrated two books by Peter Geibler including *Yours and Mine*. Almud lives in Munich.

Gunilla Kvarnström was born in 1946 in
Sweden. She has been working as an illustrator for thirty years and is well renowned in Sweden for her work on children's books.

Sergio Lairla was born in 1960. Since
1981 he has attempted to combine his two big passions: music and photography, and in 1991 he published his first story. He has been writing since he was shown how to join up letters and his stories always carry a message, which can help children as they grow up.

Aurélie Lanchais was born in Paris, France.
She studied art in Orleans and has designed toys and colouring books. She is the co-author of the *Who am I? What am I?* series with Alain Crozon.

Lena and Olof Landström a husband
and wife team, were both born in 1943 in Sweden and began their careers as cartoonists and film-makers. Their 'Will' picture book series created in the 1990s have received much critical acclaim. They have worked on many projects together and a number of their animated films have become genuine classics.

André Letria was born in 1973 in Lisbon,
Portugal. After studying at the Faculty of Fine Arts in Lisbon, he has worked as an illustrator since 1992, illustrating over 25 books. André has taken part in national and international exhibitions, the most important ones being the Lisbon Illustration and Comic Strip Show (from 1998 – 2001), the *Biennial of Illustration Bratislava* (1995) and the Bologna International Book Fair Exhibition (2003). He was awarded the Portuguese *National Book Illustration Prize* in 2000.

José Jorge Letria was born in 1951 in
Cascais, Portugal. He is a journalist and writer and has written over 30 children's books and over 20 anthologies of poems. He has worked on many picture books together with his son André Letria.

Eric L'Homme was born in 1967 in
Grenoble, France and grew up in the Drôme region of France. He has a Master's in history, is a nature lover and has travelled a lot, especially in central Asia, Pakistan, Afghanistan and the Philippines. Eric works as a journalist and editor of environmental magazine *Jeunes pour la Nature*. *The Book of the Stars* trilogy is his first novel. The first volume *Quadehar the Sorcerer* won the *Saint-Dié-des-Vosges Prix Jeunesse du Festival International*

Biographies

de Géographie in 2001 and the second volume, *The Mystery of Lord Sha* won the *Var Schoolchildren's Prize*. He lives in the Drôme.

Inger Lindahl was born in 1953 in Sweden. She has been working as a teacher and lives in Gothenburg. Her books about Zigge received the Swedish Booksellers' Prize.

Astrid Lindgren (1907-2002) was born in 1907 in Vimmerby, Sweden. She started writing in 1944 and her first book was *Britt-Mari finds herself*. Shortly after, Pippi Longstocking was created and she established her reputation as a children's author. In the year after the first book was published in 1945, Astrid became a children's books editor with the Stockholm publishers Raban and Sjøren. Between 1945 and 1970 she wrote over 50 books including 'Pippi' sequels, picture books, plays and film scripts.

Barbro Lindgren was born in 1937 in Sweden and has produced everything from point-and-say books to picture books and books for children and young adults. Many of her works have been translated. She has worked with Eva Eriksson and Olof Landström.

Eva Lindström was born in 1952 in Sweden. She is a renowned Swedish artist and has made animated films. She received the *Elsa Beskow Plaque* in 1995.

Karin Littlewood was born and grew up in Yorkshire. She graduated from the University of Northumbria with a B.A. in graphic design, going on to do an M.A. in illustration at Manchester, and she has been illustrating ever since. Karin's first book was *Lonely Whale* and she has illustrated many titles since then including *Gemma and the Broody Hen*, *Billy's Sunflower* and *Sun Slices, Moon Slices*.

Ana Maria Machado was born in Brazil and is one of the world's most distinguished writers for children. Not only has she won the *Hans Christian Andersen Award* in 2000, she was elected to the Brazilian Academy of Letters – the first writer for children to be so honoured. She has won numerous other awards. Her book *Me in the Middle* was on the 2002 Americas Award Commended List.

Henning Mankell was born in 1948 in Stockholm and is one of Sweden's best-selling authors. He has published a number of plays and novels for adults, many of them drawing on his own experiences in Africa. Henning is well known internationally for his series of crime novels about inspector Kurt Wallander which has generated numerous international film and television adaptations. His books for children and young adults have won him several awards, including the prestigious *Astrid Lindgren Prize* in 1996. He won the *German Youth Book Prize* in 1993 for *A Bridge to the Stars*. He now divides his time between Sweden and Maputo, Mozambique, where he works as the director of *Teatro Avenida*. He is passionately committed to the fight against AIDS in Africa.

Alan Marks was born in 1957 and grew up in Docklands, London. When he left school he was already passionate about drawing and went to Medway College of Art and Design in Kent, and later to art college in Bath. After returning to London to work for newspapers and magazines, he occasionally returned to Bath to teach. He also taught at art college in Southampton. Alan has illustrated many picture books and won the Carnegie Medal in 1985. He lives in Kent.

Nina Matthis was born in 1961 in Sweden. She has been working as a journalist, a teacher and as therapist. Nina is the author of *The Grandma Hunt* and lives just outside Stockholm.

André Maurois (1885-1967) – a pseudonym of Émile Salomon Wilhelm Herzog – was born in France in 1885. `Maurois' was the name of a village near where he was stationed in the First World War as a liaison officer with the British Army. He was a biographer, novelist, essayist and children's writer. His first book was *The Silence of Colonel Bramble* 1918, a collection of essays about British life. Maurois is best known for his vivid and romantic style biographies of Shelley, Byron, Balzac, Proust and others.

Diana Mayo studied Graphic Design and Illustration at Kingston University, Surrey. After graduating in 1990 she became a freelance illustrator working with several publishers illustrating children's books, including *Gingerbread Man*, *House That Jack Built* and *Winter King and the Summer Queen.* Diana often holds an 'open studio' to give advice to new illustrators and she runs courses on children's book illustration.

Kai Meyer was born in 1969 in Germany. He started out as a trainee journalist for a newspaper. It was during his two years as a staff journalist that he developed his writing skills and cultivated his talent for fast-paced action writing. Kai's debut novel *The Flowing Queen* is the first part of a trilogy and has sold over a quarter of a million hardback copies in Germany.

Kerstin Meyer was born in 1966 near Hamburg, Germany. She studied illustration at Hamburg College of Design and has worked as an illustrator for several publishers of children's books as well as for television.

Brigitte Minne is a Belgian author and has written several successful picture books including *The Best Bottom*. Brigitte lives in Belgium.

Birte Müller was born in 1973 in Hamburg, Germany. After leaving school she travelled for six months in Australia and in 1995 enrolled at the Institute of Higher Education in Hamburg. Her work has been shown in joint and individual exhibitions and in 1999 her children's book illustrations were chosen for an exhibition and catalogue of the international Bologna Children's Book Fair. Birt's first picture book was published in 2001. She lives in Hamburg.

Marie-Aude, Lorris and Elvire Murail are France's most famous literary siblings and were born in Le Havre in the Seine-Maritime, France. They are all widely published novelists. Marie-Aude studied at the Sorbonne and has written several books for children under the pseudonym Moka, selling over two million books worldwide. Elvire studied at Cambridge and published her first novel for adults in 1983 which was turned into a film and has won several literary awards. She began writing for children in 1989, and has written over fifty books as well as working as a scriptwriter for cinema and television. Lorris is well known for writing about his two passions: good food and science fiction.

Aziz Nesin (1915-1995) was born in 1915 in Istanbul, Turkey. He was one of Turkey's most popular writers and his novels and short stories cover an impressive range of subjects and are animated by his unique and satirical wit. He won numerous literary awards and in 1972 he established the charitable Nesin Foundation to fund the education and care of homeless and destitute children.

Per Nilsson was born in 1954 in Malmö, Sweden. He worked as a maths and music teacher before becoming a writer in 1999. He is one of Sweden's leading authors of young people's literature. *Heart's Delight (Loves Me Loves Me Not)* was awarded the *German Literature Children's Prize* in 1997. Per was honoured for his work with the *Astrid Lindgren Prize* in 1999. He lives with his wife and four children in Sölvesborg, a small village on Sweden's Baltic coast.

Michel Noël grew up in the logging camps of northern Quebec, Canada, living alongside the Algonquian of Lac Rapide, Lac Victoria and Maniwaki where his father worked for an international paper company. He is the author of several award-winning books for young people, including *La ligne de trappe*, which won the *Governor General's Award* and the *Prix Alvine Belisle* for the best children's book published in Quebec. He now lives in Quebec City where he works in the Ministry of Culture and Communications as co-ordinator of native affairs.

Carl Norac was born in 1960 in Mons, Belgium, the son of a writer and an actress. His family left the city to live in the middle of the forest and the importance of nature in his books comes from his early years spent wandering among the trees. Carl worked in a number of different fields as a French teacher, a television scriptwriter and a journalist before devoting himself completely to his passion, writing. In addition to poetry and plays, he has written numerous children's books. Some of these, such as *Les mots doux* (*I Love You So Much*), have been translated into 18 different languages with worldwide success.

Sofia Nordin studied at the University of Stockholm and is an occasional maths and science teacher. *In the Wild* is her first children's book and won the Eriksson and Lindgren 2002 'The Joy of Storytelling Competition'. She has just completed her second book, *Natanhuset*, and has also written a novel for adults. She lives in Stockholm, Sweden.

Christine Nöstlinger was born in 1936 in Austria. After working as a journalist, she had her breakthrough as an author in 1970. Now she is one of the most acclaimed authors of books for children and young people. She has written for TV and radio productions as well. Christine has received numerous prizes and awards including the *German Youth Literature Prize* in 1973, the *Hans Christian Andersen Medal* from IBBY in 1984 and the *Astrid Lindgren Memorial Award* in 2003. She has become an international author with many of her books translated into English.

Helena Olofsson HeshmatPasand was born in 1957 in northern Sweden. She is an artist and writer and has written several children's books including *The Little Jester*. Helena lives in Stockholm.

Gudrun Pausewang was born in 1928 in Germany. She is a distinguished author of many teenage novels in her native Germany. *The Final Journey* won the *Marsh Award for Children's Literature in Translation* in 1999. Gudrun has also won the *Gustav-Heinemann Peace Prize*, the *German Youth Literature Prize* and the *Birmingham Children's Book Award*.

Daniel Pennac was born in 1944 in Casablanca, Morocco. He has travelled widely, working at various times as a woodcutter, a cab driver and an illustrator, before finally becoming a teacher. He has spent thirty years working with children with emotional and learning difficulties. One of the most translated authors in France, his books for both adults and children appear in over thirty different languages. The Kamo stories in particular are extremely popular. Daniel lives in Paris.

Moritz Petz was born in 1975 in Munich, Germany. He spent his childhood in the very inspiring craft studio (Kunstwerkstatt) of his grandparents. After leaving school he travelled for some time through Italy, Denmark and Sweden where he had various jobs. He is interested in street and puppet theatre, chess, music and of course writing, especially children's books. He lives in the south of Germany.

Marcus Pfister was born in 1960 in Berne, Switzerland. After leaving school he took a foundation course at the art school in Berne and afterwards studied as a graphic designer. From 1981 to 1983 he worked in advertising in Zurich. He is the author and illustrator of many popular books about Penguin Pete and Milo and is the creator of the international best-selling Rainbow Fish books. Marcus received the Bologna Book Fair *Critici in Erba Prize*, the *Christopher Award*, and the 1995 *American Booksellers' Book of the Year Award* for the Rainbow Fish series. He lives in Switzerland with his wife, two sons and daughter.

Marjolein Pottie is a Belgian artist who has become well-known and respected as a European illustrator. She illustrated *The Best Bottom* by Brigitte Minne. Marjolein lives in Belgium.

Markéta Prachatická is an award-winning artist from the Czech Republic. She has illustrated books by Roger McGough and Roald Dahl (including the Czech edition of *James and the Giant Peach*) and won the prestigious *Premio Grafico Prize* at the Bologna Children's Book Fair for *Alice in Wonderland*.

Mirjam Pressler was born in Darmstadt, Germany. She is an award-winning author of several novels for young people. A highly regarded expert on the life of Anne Frank, she was the editor of the *Definitive Edition of Anne Frank: The Diary of a Young Girl* , translator of the Diary from Dutch into German and she is also the author of *The Story of Anne Frank*. Mirjam was awarded the *Volkacher Taler*, the *Carl-Zuckmayer Medal* and the *German Book Award* for her literary work as a whole, and her work as a translator won the

special prize of the *German Youth Literature Award*. She lives in the Bavarian countryside.

Anne Provoost was born in 1964 in Belgium and studied literature and education at the University of Leuven. Her first novel was *My Aunt is a Pilot Whale* published in 1991 while she was living in Minnesota in the USA. Her second novel, *Falling* was made into a film. She is the author of four novels that have together been translated into ten languages, and won twelve major awards. Anne was elected a member of the Royal Academy of Dutch Language and Literature in 2003. She lives in Antwerp with her husband and three children.

Sirish Rao has written a number of children's books and also co-authored (with Gita Wolf) a book of retellings of several myths and fables, *Antigone,* which won several international awards. He wrote his first novel, *Real Men Don't Pick Peonies* at the age of 22. Sirish is part of the core editorial team of Tara Publications.

Anushka Ravishankar is the author of over ten books of verse, fiction, and non-fiction and is considered a pioneer of the Indian English nonsense verse form and has written several such successful volumes, including *Anything but a Grabooberry* and *Catch that Crocodile*.

Bjarne Reuter was born in 1950 and grew up in a working-class environment in Brønshøj, Denmark. Following various casual jobs, he trained as a teacher, qualifying in 1975 and taught until 1980 when he became a full-time writer. He published his first book, *Kidnapping*, in 1975 and is currently one of the most frequently and widely translated Danish authors of children's literature.

Biographies

Sibylle and Jürgen Rieckhoff are a husband and wife team who live and work in Germany. Sibylle studied illustration and worked in advertising and graphic design before writing her first children's book in 1999. Jürgen worked as a cartoonist and illustrator for 11 years and is now a Professor of Drawing in Dessau.

Marlies Rieper-Bastian was born in 1946 near Bielefeld, Germany. She studied graphic design at technical college in Bielefeld and then worked as a graphic designer in advertising. Since 1974 she has also worked as a freelance illustrator for children's magazines, non-fiction books and school textbooks as well as illustrating her own children's books. Marlies lives with her husband in Braunschweig, Germany.

Alessandra Roberti was born in 1971 in Italy. She obtained a diploma from the Art Institute of Urbino followed by a diploma in painting from the Art Academy of Florence. She collaborated with different Italian publishers and took part in various exhibitions in different Italian cities. Alessandra lives and works between Tuscany and the Marche region where she teaches Art and Design.

Martha Sandwall-Bergström (1913-2000) was born in 1913 in Småland, Sweden. Her books have sold over four million copies world-wide and have been translated into twelve languages. The Goldie books are based on her own experiences of growing up in a poor area in Sweden.

Marjane Satrapri was born in 1969, in Rasht, Iran. She grew up in Tehran where she studied at the Lycée Français before leaving for Vienna. She then went on to study illustration in Strasbourg. Marjana is the author of several children's books and her illustrations appear regularly in newspapers and magazines. She now lives in Paris.

Emanuele Scanziani was born in Italy and is an artist and freelance illustrator who lives and works in Auroville, an international commune in South India. He has illustrated several books in a range of styles including the comic form and he is the illustrator of the *Legend of the Fish* by Gita Wolf and Sirish Rao.

Ron Schröder was born in the Netherlands. He works for Dutch television and started writing children's stories, songs for magazines, radio programmes and television shows, together with his partner, Marianne Busser. They live together with their three daughters, Anne, Jette and Liselotje, in the Netherlands.

Ingrid and Dieter Schubert a husband and wife team, were both born and raised in Germany. After studying art at the Academy of Design in Münster and the Academy of Art in Düsseldorf they moved to Amsterdam to study at the Gerrit Rietveld Academy. They are the creators of many award-winning picture books for children and their first book, *There's a Crocodile Under my Bed!* was an immediate success and was published in 14 countries. Ingrid and Dieter have won several awards including a National Parenting Publications Gold Award for *Amazing Animals* and a *Golden Brush* award for *Where is My Monkey?* They live in Amsterdam.

Bhajju Shyam was born in India. Like most children in his Gond village, he grew up helping his mother paint the walls of their home. Bhajju's family were too poor to keep him on in school, so when he turned 16, he went to the city of Bhopal in search of work, taking several odd jobs before becoming an artist's apprentice. In 2001 he received a state award for Best Indigenous Artist and his work has been exhibited in the UK, Germany, Holland and Russia. Bhajju lives and works in Bhopal, central India.

André Sollie was born in 1947 in Mechelen, Belgium, and studied at the Saint Lucas Institute in Brussels. He began his career making commercial designs, cartoons, and occasional graphics, and later specialised in layout and illustrations. He has illustrated over 200 covers and books including the series of Top-books for teenagers and his first volume of verses, *Soms dan heb ik flink de pest in* (*Sometimes I really feel fed up*).

Angela Sommer-Bodenburg was born in Reinbek, near Hamburg, Germany. She studied education, psychology and sociology at the University of Hamburg in 1972 and was a teacher for 12 years. Since 1984 she has been a freelance writer and painter and has written more than 40 books including poetry, picture books, novels and 18 books in the 'Little Vampire' series. Angela lives in Silver City, New Mexico with her husband and two Hungarian sheepdogs.

Anu Stohner was born in Helsinki and is a freelance translator and author. She is the author of *Santa's Littlest Helper* and lives in Munich.

Véronique Tadjo grew up in Abidjan on the Ivory Coast and studied for her BA in English before going on to study at the Sorbonne, Paris, where she earned her doctorate. In 1983, she went to Howard University in Washington D.C. on a Fulbright research scholarship. In addition to her children's books, she has written books of poetry and essays, which have won numerous awards, and has edited anthologies of African writing. She is currently based in Johannesburg, South Africa, where she continues to paint and write.

Lilli Thal is a historian and author. She established herself in the German children's book market with her prize-winning series of humorous crime stories about Inspector Pillermeier. Lilli lives in southern Germany with her husband, two children and a dog.

Raphaël Thierry lives in Paris, France, where he divides his time between creating children's books, graphic design and painting. He is the author of the 'Superdog Adventure' series of picture books and has recently won a prestigious grant from the French Ministry of Culture to work at the Académie de France in Rome.

Marit Törnqvist was born in Uppsala, Sweden, and moved to the Netherlands when she was five years old. After completing her studies in Illustration at the Amsterdam Rietveld Academy, she returned to Sweden where she collaborated with author Astrid Lindgren on four picture books, including *The Red Bird*. She has also designed scenery based on Astrid Lindgren's work for the Junibacken fairy-tale house in Stockholm. She was selected for the IBBY Honour List in 2000 for her illustrations for *Helden op sokken* by Annie Makkink. She now lives and works in Amsterdam.

Michel Tournier is a highly respected journalist, broadcaster and author of numerous books for adults and children. His first novel, *Friday*, was published to international critical acclaim and won the *Grand Prix du roman* of the Académie française. After the success of this adult version of the classic Robinson Crusoe tale, Michel decided to share his research and enthusiasm for the story with younger readers and *Friday and Robinson* was an immediate success when it was first published in 1971. The author's second adult novel, *Le Roi des Aulnes*, was the first book ever to be the unanimous

Biographies

winner of the *Prix Goncourt*, France's most prestigious literary award. Michel lives in France.

Eugene Trivizas was born in Greece. He is one of Greece's best-loved authors for children and has written over one hundred books, all currently in print. His first book for children published in the English language *The Three Little Wolves and the Big Bad Pig* has been translated into 12 languages. Eugene has been named the winner of 20 national and international literary prizes and awards, and much of his work has been adapted for stage, screen and radio. He is a barrister-at-law and a professor of criminology, teaching international and comparative criminology at the Universities of Reading, England and Athens, Greece.

Hervé Tullet was born in 1958 in France. He studied art and advertising and worked for ten years as a director for an advertising company. He published his first children's book in 1994 and is also an illustrator for *Le Monde*, *Libération*, *Elle* and *The New Yorker*. He is known as the 'Prince of preschool books in France' and has won several prizes. Many of his books have been translated into English, including *Pink Lemon* and *Night and Day* and more recently he has collaborated with Michael Rosen on *The Alphabet Poem*.

Sedat Turhan conceived and developed the popular Milet picture dictionary range and is Director of Milet Publishing and he has been the main distributor of Turkish books in Britain for over 20 years. Prior to setting up his distribution and publishing companies, he worked in education and youth support for the Turkish community.

Guido van Genechten has won several prizes for his children's book illustrations. He lives and works in Belgium.

Ted van Lieshout was born in 1955 Eindhoven, the Netherlands, and he attended the Rietveld Academy in Amsterdam, where he studied illustration and graphic design. After graduating in 1980, he worked for various publishers, designing book covers and illustrating for newspapers and magazines. In 1982 he started illustrating for a literary magazine for children; he published his first poetry and stories in it two years later, and started writing for the Dutch version of the television programme *Sesame Steet* the very same year. In 1986, his first two books were published: the story *Raven's Travelling Theatre* and the volume of children's poetry *You Can Fold Sorrow into Funny Hats*. Ted lives in Amsterdam.

Sylvia van Ommen was born in 1978 in the Netherlands and went to the Academy of Art in Kampen. She illustrates and writes about everything she sees and hears around her and is one of the most promising and original young illustrators working in the Netherlands. Her books have been published in Germany, France, Mexico, Japan and the United States.

Max Velthuijs (1923-2005) was born in 1923 in The Hague, the Netherlands. He studied graphic design and art at the Academy in Arnhem, Holland. He had a very successful career as a graphic designer, making political prints, cartoons, posters and book jackets and working on animated films and advertisements, for which he received many international awards. These included the *Dutch Silver Pencil Award* and *Dutch Golden Paintbrush Award* (twice), the *American Graphic Award* of the Society of Illustrators, the French *Prix de Treize* and the German *Bestlist Award* (also twice). He only began his full-time career as an author and illustrator for the young when he was aged 60. His first picture book *The Boy and the Fish* appeared in 1967. He had many one-man exhibitions in Dutch galleries. Max was best known for his series of international best-selling Frog books for which he was awarded the *Hans Christian Andersen Award* in 2004.

Buket Uzuner was born in 1955 in Turkey. She trained as a biologist and environmental scientist, studying and working at universities in Turkey, Norway, Finland and the USA. She is one of Turkey's best-selling authors and has published short story collections, novels and works of travel writing. Her novel *Kumral Ada Mavi Tuna* has been a bestseller in Turkey since its release in 1997 and was named the Best Novel of 1998 by the University of Istanbul. It has been translated into English (*Mediterranean Waltz*), Italian, Greek and Hebrew.

Uli Waas was born in 1949 in Donauwörth, southern Germany. She studied painting and graphic arts at the Academy of Fine Arts in Munich. For several years she has been writing stories for children's books and illustrating them in pastels and gouache and she likes to illustrate children's books with animals as the main characters. Uli lives with her husband, their two children and a Jack Russell terrier on the edge of the Swabian Alps.

Steve Weatherill was born in 1951, in Scarborough, North Yorkshire, UK. He studied Fine Art at Hornsey College of Art, followed by an MA in Film and Television at the Royal College of Art. Steve worked as an illustrator and cartoonist in London and drew a weekly cartoon strip in the *Financial Times* called 'The Rat Race', and has illustrated many children's books including the 'Baby Goz' series. Steve lives in South Lincolnshire with his wife, two sons and two geese.

Fritz Wegner was born in 1924 in Vienna, Austria, but was naturalised as a British subject. He studied at St. Martins School of Art from 1939 to 1942, and later became a guest lecturer. He eventually began doing freelance work, which included exhibition design for the Ministry of Agriculture royal shows. Fritz's professional career has encompassed stamp design, advertising for English and American clients, and illustrations in books (including children's books), magazines and periodicals.

Ilon Wikland was born in 1930 in Estonia and went to Sweden as a 14-year-old refugee. She studied as an artist in Sweden and started collaborating with Astrid Lindgren in 1954. Ilon illustrated most of Astrid's books and she has received numerous prizes and awards. In 1969 she was awarded the *Elsa Beskow Plaque* for her collected works. Now she writes and illustrates her own books.

Henrike Wilson was born in Cologne, Germany and studied graphic design and painting there and in the USA. She is the illustrator of *Santa's Littlest Helper* by Anu Stohner.

Gita Wolf is one of the most original and creative voices in contemporary Indian publishing. She trained as an academic in English and Comparative Literature and has written over a dozen books for children and adults, of which several have been honoured with international awards, including the Alcuin Citation in Canada in 1997 for *The Very Hungry Lion* and the 1999 *Biennale of Illustration Bratislava* plaque in 1999 for *Hen-sparrow Turns Purple*. She already has a repertoire of retellings to her name, including the rendition (with Sirish Rao) of Sophocles' *Antigone*. In 1994 she set up Tara Publications, a small independent publishing house run by a group of writers based in Chennai, India.

Kazumi Yumoto was born in 1959 in Tokyo, Japan. While studying musical composition at Tokyo University of Music she wrote scripts for operas. After graduation she wrote for radio and television. Her first young adult novel, *The Friends,* was made into a film and radio play in 1994 and won the *Mildred L. Batchelder Award* for Translation and the *Boston Globe-Horn Book Award* for Fiction in 1997. It was also named an ALA Notable Children's Book and won the Recommended Book Prize from Japan School Library Book Club. Kazumi lives in Tokyo.

Valérie Zenatti was born in 1970, in Nice, France. When she was 13, she went to live in Israel with her parents, where she did her national service, which inspired her novel *When I was a Soldier*. She now lives in Paris with her two young children where she works as a translator of Hebrew.

Reiner Zimnik was born in 1930, in Beuthen, Upper Silesia, Poland. At the end of the Second World War, he and his family left for the West, settling in Munich, Germany. After training as a carpenter, he studied at the Academy of Fine Arts where he wrote and designed *The Crane*, published in 1956.

Translators

Sarah Adams (see pages 12 and 93)

Pelin Arıner was born in 1976 in Ankara, Turkey. The daughter of a diplomat, she has followed her parents around the world living in Sudan, Greece and Turkey. After receiving degrees in both creative writing and double bass performance from Oberlin College, Ohio, she decided that there was nothing that she would rather do than translate the books of her favourite Turkish writer, Buket Uzuner. Pelin lives in the USA.

Anthea Bell was born in Suffolk and educated at Somerville College, Oxford, England. She has worked for many years as a translator, mainly from German and French (but also Danish and Dutch), with some two hundred titles translated including all the Asterix books. Anthea has translated many works for both adults and young people and won numerous awards for her work: a Certificate of Honour in the Hans Christian Andersen translators' honour list (three times), the *Mildred L. Batchelder Award* (twice), the 1987 *Schlegel-Tieck Prize* and the *Astrid Lindgren Prize*. In 1996 Anthea won the first *Marsh Award for Children's Literature in Translation* for Christine Nöstlinger's *A Dog's Life* and again in 2003 for *Where Were You Robert?* by Hans Magnus Enzensberger and was also shortlisted for her translation of Reinhardt Jung's *Bambert's Book of Missing Stories.* More recently she has translated Hervé Jubert's *Dance of the Assassins* and *Devil's Tango*, Cornelia Funke's *Inkheart* and *Dragon Rider*, and Kai Meyer's *The Flowing Queen*.

John Brownjohn is one of Britain's foremost translators from German. He has translated many books and screenplays into English from German and French, including books by Leo Perutz and Thomas Brussig. John has won the *Schlegel-Tieck*

Prize twice, for his translations of *The Swedish Cavalier* by Leo Perutz and *Infanta* by Bodo Kirchoff.

Linda Coverdale was born in the USA and learned French at the age of ten, when her parents moved to Grenoble for a year and went on to study French at Johns Hopkins University. She has translated many works from French into English and has won numerous awards including the *American Foundation's Translation Prize* in 1997 for her translation of *Literature of Life* by Jorge Semprun, the Knight of the Order of Arts and Letters from France in 2001 for her significant role in promoting French literature and thought in the United States and *The International IMPAC Dublin Literary Award* for *This Blinding Absence of Light* by Tahar Ben Jelloun in 2004.

Patricia Crampton was born in India and was bilingual in Hindi and English from her early years. She read Modern Languages at Oxford (German, French and one year of Russian). Her early work included translating at the Nuremberg War Crimes Trials and being the conference organiser and translator for NATO Parliamentarians (Westminster). Patricia has translated several children's books, including Gudrun Pausewang's *Final Journey* which won the *Marsh Award for Children's Literature in Translation* in 1999 and *No Roof in Bosnia* by Els de Groen which was shortlisted in the same year. Awards also include the *Astrid Lindgren Prize*, the *Schlegel-Tieck Prize* and, in 1991, the *Eleanor Farjeon Award* for her services to children's literature. Patricia has been actively involved in the Translators Association, IBBY (International Board on Books for Young People) and has been jury chairman of the *Hans Christian Andersen Prize*.

Damian Croft was born in 1966, in Preston, Lancashire. After a degree in music he spent several years working as a jazz musician in London before taking up teaching English in Ankara, Turkey. He returned to the UK in 1994 to work as an English teacher in Haringey and Enfield where he developed close ties with the Turkish communities there. When not translating and teaching, Damian works as a writer of fiction. He lives in Sicily, Italy.

Phoebe Dunn was born in 1971 in Crowborough, East Sussex. She studied at Worcester College, Oxford and translated *How to Talk to Children About Art* from French by Françoise Barbe Gall. Phoebe lives in North London.

Elisabeth Kallick Dyssegaard was born in 1963 in Demark. She is an editor of adult books and has translated many children's books from Swedish for R&S Books. She lives in New York City, USA.

Tom Geddes taught Swedish and German at the University College of Wales, Aberystwyth, before becoming head of the Germanic collections at the British Library. He has translated 20 books from Swedish or Norwegian, written articles on Swedish literature and contributed reviews and bibliographies to *Scandinavica, Swedish Book Review* and other journals. His translation of *The Way of a Serpent* by Torgny Lindgren won the *Bernard Shaw Prize for Swedish Translation* in 1991, and in 1992 he received the Royal Order of the Polar Star from Sweden for his services to Swedish literature. He was awarded the *Swedish Academy Translation Prize* in 2002

Sarah Jane Hails was born in 1970 in Rothbury, Northumberland. She studied Scandinavian Studies majoring in Norwegian at the University of East Anglia and Modern Languages and a Postgraduate teaching certificate at the University of Oslo. She met

Jostein Gaarder in 1992 and did a sample translation of *The Solitaire Mystery* as part of a university assignment. In 1994 Sarah was awarded a scholarship from the Norwegian Research Council to research and translate Norwegian Children's and Youth Literature. The translation of *The Solitaire Mystery* was completed in 1996, followed by a poem by Sigbjørn Obstfelder, *Rain,* in the poetry collection *Around the World in Eighty Poems*. Sarah lives in Norway and now works for the Norwegian Government as an editor of their national information portal.

Michael Henry Heim is Professor of Slavic Languages and Literatures and Comparative Literature at the University of California, Los Angeles. He translates contemporary and classic fiction and drama from Russian, Czech, French, German, Serbian/Croatian, Hungarian, Italian and Romanian. He has been the recipient of numerous awards, including the *Helen and Kurt Wolff Translator's Prize* for his translation of Thomas Mann's *Death in Venice* in 2005.

Cathy Hirano is a professional translator from Japanese into English. She has translated many children's books including picture books and is the translator of Kazumi Yumoto's books including *Letters From the Living.* Cathy won the *Mildred L. Batchelder Award* for translation in 1997 for Kazumi Yumoto's young adult novel, *The Friends*.

Neal Hoskins (see pages 21 and 94)

Adriana Hunter spent four years at a French school as a child and took a degree in French and Drama at the University of London. She worked as a film publicist and freelance writer before turning to translating. She has now translated over 20 books including works by Agnès Desarthe, Amélie Nothomb, Frédéric Beigbeder and Catherine Millet and has twice been shortlisted for the *Independent Foreign Fiction Prize*. Her most recent children's book translation is *When I was a Soldier*.

J. Alison James was born in southern California, but she has lived all over the world. She received a degree in English and languages from Vassar College, and a master's degree from The Centre for the Study of Children's Literature in Boston. Her first novel, *Sing for a Gentle Rain* was published in 1990 and she has been writing and translating books for children ever since. She has published two picture books and two novels for young adults and she has translated more than 130 books for children, mostly from German, but also from Swedish and Japanese. She lives with her husband and daughter in northern Vermont.

Asha Kathoria wrote the Hindi text for the dual-language book *Chanda and the Mirror of Moonlight* by Margaret Bateson Hill. Asha was born and grew up in India where she qualified with an M.A. in Sanskrit from Delhi University. She speaks Hindi as a first language, as well as Punjabi and Urdu. Her stories have been published in popular Hindi magazines and she has also worked as a teacher in India and Zambia. Asha obtained a postgraduate diploma in Librarianship from Thames Valley University in London. She also qualified as a Chartered Librarian and until recently worked as a children's librarian for the Education Library Service, Berkshire.

Marianne Martens has translated over 100 books into English, mainly from German. She has worked in publishing for 18 years, and has taught Publishing for Young Readers at City College in New York. She served as the US Juror for the Hans Christian Andersen Award in 2002 and 2004. Marianne speaks Danish, English, German, French and Spanish, and also reads Swedish and Norwegian. She is currently working on her MLIS degree at the University of Illinois.

Brian Murdoch is Professor of German at Stirling University in Scotland and has held Visiting Fellowships at Cambridge and Oxford. He is the author of many books and articles on medieval and modern German and has published several translations, including *All Quiet on the Western Front* by Remarque and, in collaboration with Mike Mitchell, the autobiography of Erwin Blumenfeld, *Eye to I*. He has translated two children's books by Mirjam Pressler from the German, *Shylock's Daughter* and *Malka*.

John Nieuwenhuizen was born in the Netherlands and emigrated to Australia in 1955. He spent 17 years teaching in Australian secondary schools, and has since worked as a public and school librarian. He has been active in establishing The Australian Literary Translators Association and has translated many books from the Dutch language including *A Mouthful of Feathers* by Lydia Rood, *The Baboon King* by Anton Quintana, which won the *Mildred L. Batchelder Award* for outstanding literature in translation in 1999 and two novels by Anne Provoost, *Falling* and *In the Shadow of the Ark*. John lives in Melbourne, Australia.

Tiina Nunnally is from Seattle, USA. At the age of 17 she went to Denmark as an exchange student for a year and went on to study English at Western Washington University and then did postgraduate studies in Scandinavian literature. Tiina translates books from both Danish and Norwegian and her first translation, a memoir by the Danish author, Tove Ditlevsen, won a translation prize from the American Scandinavian Foundation. One of the most recent books that Tiina has translated into English is *Fairy Tales: Hans Christian Andersen* edited by Jackie Wullschager. She lives in West Seattle.

Doris Orgel was born in Vienna, Austria and went to the USA as a child. She is an author and translator who has translated and retold many fairy and folk tales as well as writing picture books and novels for young adults. Her first book, *Sarah's Room,* published in 1963, was illustrated by Maurice Sendak. She is best known for her novel *The Devil in Vienna* based on her childhood experiences in 1930s Austria.

Anna Paterson is an award-winning translator who has translated many literary projects from Scandinavian languages and German into English and Swedish. In 2000, she won the *Bernard Shaw Prize for Swedish Translation* for her translation of *Forest of Hours* by Kerstin Ekman. Anna lives in Scotland.

Maurice Riordan has published two poetry collections with Faber and Faber. *A Word from the Loki* was nominated for the *T.S. Elliot Prize* and *Floods* was shortlisted for the *Whitbread Poetry Prize* in 2000. Maurice translated and adapted one of the first picture book titles to be published by WingedChariot Press, *The Moon Has Written You a Poem* by José Jorge. He has recently been working with Maltese writers on another translation project.

Betsy Rosenberg was born in Philadelphia, Pennsylvania in 1946 and lived in Haifa, Israel from 1948-1956. She attended the Rubin Academy of Music and the Hebrew University, studying musicology, literature, theatre and comparative linguistics and also took a radio acting course at the Israel Broadcasting Authority where she first met David Grossman. Betsy worked as a singer, flautist and actress and performed in radio plays for children before taking up translation in 1973. She has translated several books by David Grossman including *Duel* which won the *Marsh Award for Children's Literature in Translation* in 2001. As well as working as a translator, Betsy is a freelance editor, writer and teacher of creative writing. She lives in Indiana.

Lance Salway is the author of over 25 books for children and reviews and criticism of children's literature in *Signal*, *TLS*, *The Guardian* and many other journals. He has translated over 20 children's books from Dutch into English as well as non-fiction for adults. His translation of *Brothers* by Ted van Lieshout was shortlisted for the 2003 *Marsh Award for Children's Literature in Translation*.

Joan Sandin was born in 1942 in Watertown, Wisconsin, USA. She graduated from the University of Arizona with a BFA in Art. She is an author, illustrator and translator and has translated several children's books from Swedish to English for R&S Books.

Ros Schwartz dropped out of university and ran away to Paris in the '70s. She has been a full-time freelance translator since 1981 and has translated a wide range of fiction and non-fiction from French, in particular contemporary North African authors. She is actively involved in the Translators Association and in the British Centre for Literary Translation, and gives frequent workshops and talks on the art of translation. When translating teenage fiction, she works closely with her own two teenagers, Leo and Chloe, and is grateful to them for keeping her abreast of teen slang.

Anne Connie Stuksrud was born in Norway but has lived and studied in Australia since 1996. She has published two short story collections for young adults in Scandinavia.

Laurie Thompson was born in 1938 in York. He studied German at the University of Manchester, lived in Sweden for some years in the 1960s and edited *Swedish Book Review* for twenty years from its launch in 1983. He has translated nearly forty books (mainly for adults) from Swedish, including five novels by Henning Mankell, the most recent of which is *A Bridge to the Stars*. Laurie has been awarded prizes by the Swedish Academy and the Swedish Writers' Association. He lives in rural West Wales with his Swedish wife and several cats.

Anna Trenter was an 'Honor Winner' of the *Mildred L. Batchelder Award* in 1998 for her translation from the German of *Hostage to War: A True Story* by Tatjana Wassiljewa. She has recently translated *Santa's Littlest Helper* by Anu Stohner and Henrike Wilson.

Hester Velmans has translated a number of novels from Dutch into English, including *The Lily Theatre* by Lulu Wang and *A Heart of Stone* by Renate Dorrestein for which she won the *Vondel Prize for Translation*. Hester's first book written for children was *Isabel of the Whales* and she has recently translated *The Dream Merchant* by Isabel Hoving.

Rachel Ward has an M.A. in Literary Translation from the University of East Anglia and has been working as a freelance translator, specialising in translation for children and young people as well as crime and other contemporary fiction. Her first translated novel was *Traitor* by Gudrun Pausewang which won the 1999 *Marsh Award for Children's Literature in Translation*.

Chantal Wright has translated children's and young adult fiction by Cornelia Funke and Zoran Drvenkar. An excerpt from her translation of Radek Knapp's *Mr Kuka's Recommendations* was published in *Two Lines: A Journal of Translation* in 2003.

Publishers

Allen and Unwin Books

(Distributed by
Frances Lincoln)

Andersen Press

20 Vauxhall Bridge Road
London SW1V 2SA
Tel: 020 7840 8701
Fax: 020 7233 6263
www.andersenpress.co.uk

b small publishing

The Book Shed
36 Leyborne Park
Kew, Surrey TW9 3HA
Tel: 020 8948 2884
Fax: 020 8948 6458
www.bsmall.co.uk

Barn Owl Books

(Distributed by Frances
Lincoln)

Bloodaxe Books

Highgreen, Tarset
Northumberland NE48 1RP
Tel: 01434 240500
Fax: 01434 240505
www.bloodaxebooks.com

Bloomsbury
Children's Books

38 Soho Square
London W1D 3HB
Tel: 020 7494 2111
Fax: 020 7434 0151
www.bloomsbury.com

Cat's Whiskers
(Orchard Books)

The Watts Publishing Group
96 Leonard Street
London EC2A 4XD
Tel: 020 7739 2929
Fax: 020 7739 2181
www.wattspub.co.uk

The Chicken House

2 Palmer Street
Frome, Somerset BA11 1DS
Tel: 01373 454488
Fax: 01373 454499
www.doublecluck.com

Egmont
Children's Books

239 Kensington High Street
London W8 6SA
Tel: 020 7761 3500
Fax: 020 7761 3510
www.egmont.co.uk

Floris Books

15 Harrison Gardens
Edinburgh
Scotland EH11 1SH
Tel: 0131 337 2372
Fax: 0131 347 9919
www.florisbooks.co.uk

Frances Lincoln

4 Torriano Mews
Torriano Avenue
London NW5 2RZ
Tel: 020 7284 4009
Fax: 020 7485 0490
www.franceslincoln.com

Granta Books

2/3 Hanover Yard
Noel Road
London N1 8BE
Tel: 020 7704 9776
Fax: 020 7354 3469
www.granta.com

Groundwood Books

(Distributed by
Bookworm Bookshop)
110 Spandina Avenue
Suite 801, Toronto
Canada M5V 2K4
www,groundwoodbooks.com

HarperCollins
Children's Books

77/85 Fulham Palace Road
London W6 8JB

Tel: 020 8741 7070
Fax: 020 8307 4199
www.harpercollins.co.uk

Hodder
Children's Books

338 Euston Road
London NW1 3BH
Tel: 020 7873 6201
Fax: 020 7873 6225
www.bookswithbite.co.uk

Jane Nissen Books

Swan House
Chiswick Mall
London W4 2PS
Tel: 020 8994 8203
Fax: 020 8742 8198

Jonathan Cape

Children's Books
Random House
61–62 Uxbridge Road
Ealing, London W5 5SA
Tel: 020 8231 6800
Fax: 020 8231 6767
www.kidsatrandomhouse.co.uk

Little Tiger Press

1 The Coda Centre
189 Munster Road
London SW6 6AW
Tel: 020 7385 6333
Fax: 020 7385 7333
www.littletigerpress.com

Macmillan
Children's Books

20 New Wharf Road
London N1 9RR
Tel: 020 7014 6000
Fax: 020 7014 6001
www.panmacmillan.com

Mantra Lingua

Global House
303 Ballards Lane
London N12 8NP
Tel: 020 8445 5123
Fax: 020 8446 7745
www.mantralingua.com

Milet Publishing

333 North Michigan Avenue
Suite 530
Chicago IL 60601 USA
Tel: 1 312 920 1828
Fax: 1 312 920 1829
www.milet.com

New York Review Books

(Distributed by Granta Books)

North-South Books

(Distributed by Ragged
Bears Ltd)

Orion Children's Books

Orion House
Upper St Martin's Lane
London WC2H 9EA
Tel: 020 7520 4318
Fax: 020 7379 6158
www.orionbooks.co.uk

Prestel Publishing Ltd

4 Bloomsbury Place
London WC1A 2QA
Tel: 020 7323 5004
Fax: 020 7636 8004
www.prestel.com

Puffin Books

80 The Strand
London WC2R 0RL
Tel: 020 7010 3000
Fax: 020 7010 6060
www.puffin.co.uk

Ragged Bears Publishing Ltd

Unit 14A Bennetts Field
Industrial Estate
Southgate Road, Wincanton
Somerset BA9 9DT
Tel: 01963 824184
Fax: 01963 31147
www.raggedbears.co.uk

R&S Books

(Distributed by Ragged
Bears Ltd)

Simon and Schuster

Africa House
64–78 Kingsway
London, WC2B 6AH
Tel: 020 7316 1900
Fax: 020 7316 0331
www.SimonSays.co.uk

Spindlewood Books

(Distributed by Ragged
Bears Ltd)

Tara Books

(Distributed by Turnaround
Publisher Service)

Walker Books

87 Vauxhall Walk
London SE11 5HJ
Tel: 020 7793 0909
Fax: 020 7587 1123
www.walkerbooks.co.uk

Weidenfeld and Nicolson

(Orion Group Publishing)
Orion House
Upper St Martin's Lane
London WC2H 9EA
Tel: 020 7520 4318
Fax: 020 7379 6158
www.orionbooks.co.uk

WingedChariot Press

7 Court Road
Tunbridge Wells
Kent TN4 8HT
Tel: 0779 1273374
www.wingedchariot.com

Zero to Ten

Evans Publishing Group
2A Portman Mansions
Chiltern Street
London W1U 6NR
Tel: 020 7487 0920
Fax: 020 7487 0921
www.evansbooks.co.uk

Distributors

Ragged Bears Ltd

Nightingale House
Queen Camel
Somerset BA22 7NN
Tel: 01935 851590
Fax: 01935 851803
www.ragged-bears.co.uk

Turnaround Publisher Service

Unit 3, Olympia Trading Estate
Coberg Road
Wood Green
London N22 6TZ
Tel: 020 8829 3000
Fax: 020 8881 5088
www.turnaround-psl-com

The Bookworm

(Bookshop selling
Groundwood Books)
1177 Finchley Road
London NW11 0AA
Tel: 020 8201 9811
Fax: 020 8201 9311
ruth.swindon@lineone.net

Magazines and Journals (printed and online)

Bookbird

Magazine of IBBY (see page 124)
Church of Ireland
College of Education
96 Upper Rathmines Road
Dublin 6, Ireland
Tel: + 35 31 4061507
Bookbirdvc@oldtown.ie
Editors: Siobhán Parkinson
and Valerie Coghlan

Published quarterly by IBBY,
Bookbird contains articles from

all over the world on all aspects of children's and young people's literature, as well as the latest events, information, prize announcements, and books on children's literature for professionals.

New Books in German

Published by British Centre for Literary Translation
c/o The Goethe-Institut
50 Princes Gate
Exhibition Road
London SW7 2PH
Tel: 020 7596 4023
Fax: 020 7594 0245
nbg@london.goethe.org
www.new-books-in-german.com

New Books in German started in 1996 and is a twice yearly journal aimed at editors who would like to publish more translations but need independent help in finding the right titles from among the thousands published each year in the German language.

PaperTigers – A Pacific Rim Voices Project

www.papertigers.org

PaperTigers is a family of websites and real-life projects that celebrate literary voices from and about the Pacific Rim and South Asia. The PaperTigers website promotes and highlights the richness of the children's book world in the region and is a useful resource for librarians, teachers, publishers and readers.

Swedish Book Review

www.swedishbookreview.com

Swedish Book Review was launched in 1983. It publishes two main issues and a supplement every year. The main aim of SBR is to present Swedish literature to the English-speaking world. It presents translated extracts from the works of Swedish writers together with an introductory article.

Transcript – The European Internet review of books and writing.

www.transcript-review.org

Transcript is a bi-monthly review of books and writing from around Europe. Its aim is to promote quality literature written in the smaller languages and to give wider circulation to material from small-language literary publications through the medium of English, French and German. Transcript is published by Literature Across Frontiers, the European programme for literary exchange and policy debate.

Words without Borders – online

magazine for international literature.
www.wordswithoutborders.org

Words without Borders undertakes to promote international communication through translation of the world's best writing, selected and translated by a distinguished group of writers, translators, and publishing professionals and publishing and promoting these works (or excerpts) on the web. They also serve as an advocacy organisation for literature in translation, producing events that feature the work of foreign writers and connecting these writers to universities and to print and broadcast media.

Grants

Arts Council England

2 Pear Tree Court
London EC1R ODS
Tel: 0845 300 6200
Fax: 020 7608 4100
www.artscouncil.org.uk

Arts Council England is the national agency for the Arts. Literary translation is eligible for funding under the Arts Council 'Grants for the Arts' programme. Priority is given to translation of contemporary fiction and poetry, although literary non-fiction titles are also eligible if they are exceptional in terms of literary and stylistic innovation. Publishers should make the application using the standard Grants for the Arts application pack (available on the website under the funding section) and are advised to contact a literature officer in their nearest Arts Council England office for further information.

Culture 2000/EUCLID

www.euclid.info/uk/Culture2000

European funding is available for international projects through the Culture 2000 programme. EUCLID is the cultural contact point in the UK, providing seminars and newsletters, including a partner search alert.

English PEN

The English Centre of International PEN
6-8 Amwell Street
London EC1R 1VQ

Tel: 020 7713 0023
Fax: 020 7837 7838
www.englishpen.org/
writersintranslation/

English PEN exists to promote
literature and its understanding;
to uphold writers' freedoms
around the world; to campaign
against the persecution and
imprisonment of writers for
stating their views; and to promote the friendly co-operation
of writers and the free exchange
of their ideas. Writers in
Translation is a programme
that awards grants to UK
publishers for the promotion
and marketing of titles in
English translation.

The Burgess Programme

French Embassy
58 Knightsbridge
London SW1X 7JT

The Burgess Programme
is designed to assist UK
publishers with translation
costs. This Programme was
launched in 1993 by the
Literature department of the
Ministry of Foreign Affairs
and it gives direct funding
to publishers to assist with
promotional or translation
costs via the Bureau du Livre
(French Embassy) in London.

Visiting Arts

www.visitingarts.org.uk/uk_
cultural_institutes.html

The Visiting Arts website
provides a list of cultural
institutes in the UK that offer
bursaries towards the cost of
translations. Some cultural
organisations in the country
of origin offer bursaries
towards the cost of translating
as do cultural departments
and embassies in London.

The Foreign Office has a list
of all foreign embassies –
www.fco.org.uk

Prizes UK

The Corneliu M Popescu Prize for European Poetry in Translation

The Poetry Society
22 Betterton Street
London WC2H 9BU
Tel: +44 020 7420 9880
Fax: +44 020 7240 4818
info@poetrysociety.org.uk
www.poetrysociety.org.uk

Named after Corneliu M
Popescu, translator of one
of Romania's leading poets,
Mihai Eminescu, this prize is
awarded biennially to a
collection of poetry which
features poetry translated
from a European language
into English.

The Independent Foreign Fiction Prize

Arts Council England
14 Great Peter St
London SW1P 3NQ
Tel: +44 020 7973 5325

The Independent Foreign
Fiction Prize is awarded
annually and it aims to
honour a great work of fiction
by a living author that has
been translated into English
from any other language and
published in the United
Kingdom.

Marsh Award for Children's Literature in Translation

The National Centre for
Research into Children's
Literature

Froebel College
Roehampton University
Roehampton Lane
London SW15 5PJ
Tel: 020 8392 3014
G.Lathey@roehampton.ac.uk

The Marsh Award for
Children's Literature in
Translation was set up in
1996 and sponsored by the
Marsh Christian Trust. It is
awarded biennially to the best
translation of a children's book
from a foreign language into
English and published in the
UK by a British publisher.
Books are accepted for
readers from 4–16 and the
translation must be from the
original work in the original
language. The award is made
to the translator of the book.

The Times Stephen Spender Prize for Poetry Translation

Administered by the Stephen
Spender Memorial Trust
The Times Stephen
Spender Prize
3 Old Wish Road, Eastbourne
East Sussex BN21 4JZ
www.stephen-spender.org

This annual competition was
launched with the aim of
encouraging school children
and young people to try their
hand at literary translation.
Entrants are invited to translate
a poem from any language,
classical or modern, into
English. There are cash prizes
in three categories – Open,
18-and-Under and 14-and-
Under – with all winning
entries published in a booklet.
For details and to read last
year's winning entries, visit
the website or email
prize@times-spender.info
for a free copy of the booklet.

Prizes International

Astrid Lindgren Prize (Canada)

International Federation
of Translators
2001 Ave Union Bureau 1108
Montreal H3A 2S9, Canada

This international translation
prize promotes the translation
of works written for children
and is awarded either for a
single translation of outstanding
quality or for the entire work of
a translator of books written
for children. The award is
made every three years.

The Astrid Lindgren Memorial Award

Swedish National Council
for Cultural Affairs
Box 7843
SE–103 98 Stockholm, Sweden
Tel: +46-8-519 264 00
Fax: +46-8-519 264 99
literatureaward@alma.se
www.alma.se

Established by the Swedish
Government in 2002, the
Astrid Lindgren Memorial
Award is given annually to
authors, illustrators and
promoters of reading whose
work reflects the spirit of
Astrid Lindgren.

Bologna Ragazzi Award (Italy)

Bologna Fiere
Piazza Costituzione 6
40128 Bologna, Italy
www.bolognafiere.it

This prestigious award is
exclusive to exhibitors at the
Bologna Children's Book Fair.
Within two categories – fiction
and non-fiction – there are
three age groups: 0–5, 6–9
and 10–16. There is also
a prize for Outstanding
Originality – 'Novità' – which
is awarded to a title that is
considered to have particularly
innovative qualities.

Hans Christian Andersen Awards

(see address for IBBY)
www.ibby.org

The Hans Christian Andersen
Awards have been given
biennially since 1956 by
an international jury from
nominations received from
IBBY sections from around the
world. The award was first
made to an author in 1956 and
an illustrator in 1966 whose
works have made an important
contribution to children's literature. The award remains the
highest international recognition
for authors and illustrators of
children's literature.

The Mildred L. Batchelder Award

The American Library
Association (ALA)
The Association for Library
Services to Children
www.ala.org

This award was set up in
1966 in honour of Mildred L.
Batchelder, a former executive
director of the Association for
Library Services to Children,
a believer in the importance
of good books for children
in translation from all parts
of the world. It is awarded
annually to an American
publisher for a children's
book considered to be the
most outstanding of those
books originally published
in a foreign country, and
subsequently translated into
English and published in the
United States.

Organisations UK

British Centre for Literary Translation (BCLT)

School of English
and American Studies
University of East Anglia
Norwich NR4 7TJ
Tel: 01603 592134/592785
bclt@uea.ac.uk
www.uea.ac.uk/eas/centres/
bclt.intro.shtml

BCLT was established in
1989 at the University of East
Anglia by the German writer
W. G. 'Max' Sebald. Its aim
is to raise the profile of
literary translation in the UK
through an imaginative and
varied programme of events,
activities, publications and
research.

British Comparative Literature Association (BCLA)

Penny Brown, BCLA Secretary
Department of French Studies
University of Manchester
Oxford Road
Manchester M13 9PL
Transcomp@uea.ac.uk

BCLA's activities include
regular publications,
conferences and an annual
translation competition
(organised jointly with BCLT).
Prizes are awarded for the
best unpublished literary
translation from any language
into English.

British Council

Literature Department
10 Spring Gardens
London SW1A 2BN
Tel: 020 7930 8466
Fax: 020 7389 6347

The British Council Literature Department promotes British and Commonwealth literature internationally, working with British Council offices overseas, and with other organisations such as universities, publishers and arts organisations. Translation is a key area of their work and they aim to facilitate dialogue between writers from other countries and writers from Britain, and to raise awareness in the UK of literature from overseas.

Centre for Literacy in Primary Education (CLPE)

Webber Street
London SE1 8QW
Tel: 020 7401 3382/3
Fax: 020 7928 4624
info@clpe.co.uk
www.clpe.co.uk

CLPE is a resource centre, which provides INSET courses for primary teachers and others concerned with language, literacy, children's literature and educational assessment. The library contains a large display of children's books, including collections of picture books, traditional stories and poetry, and there is also a teachers' reference library. CLPE also provides a variety of different publications suitable for teachers and parents.

The Children's Bookshow

Siân Williams
Tel: 020 8960 0602
Sianwilliams1@gmail.com

The Children's Bookshow was set up in 2003 by Siân Williams and is supported by Arts Council England. It is a national tour of children's writers and illustrators who perform in theatres throughout England during October and November of each year. A programme of school workshops runs alongside the tour. Each tour has a theme and has included Poetry, Folk and Fairy Tales and Translation.

Institute of Translation and Interpreting (ITI)

Fortuna House
South Fifth Street
Milton Keynes MK9 2EU
Tel: 01908 325 250
Fax: 01908 325 259
info@iti.org.uk
www.iti.org.uk

The ITI was founded in 1986 as an independent professional association of practising translators and interpreters in the UK. It aims to promote the highest standards in translating and interpreting, offering guidance to those entering the profession and advice not only to those who offer language services but also to their customers.

International Board on Books for Young People (IBBY UK)

PO Box 20875
GB – London SE22 9WQ
Tel: 020 8299 1641
ann@lazim.demon.co.uk

IBBY UK is the British section of the International Board on Books for Young People. Membership is £25.00 annually. A newsletter, *IBBYlink*, is produced three times a year and a conference is held each year in November in collaboration with the National Centre for Research in Children's Literature.

Literature Across Frontiers

Mercator Centre
University of Wales
Aberystwyth, Wales SY23 1NN
Info@lit-across-frontiers.org
www.lit-across-frontiers.
org/whatisLAF.htm

Literature Across Frontiers is based at the Mercator Centre at the University of Wales and is a programme of literary exchange and policy debate operating through partnership with European organisations engaged in the international promotion of literature and support for literary translation.

Multilingual Matters

www.multilingual-matters.com

Multilingual Matters is an international independent publishing house with lists in the areas of bilingualism, bilingual education, books for parents, second language learning, modern foreign language learning and teaching, sociolinguistics and translation. They also produce series of books on bilingualism, bilingual education, immersion education, second language learning, language policy and multi-culturalism as well as peer-reviewed academic journals and a newsletter for parents, The Bilingual Family Newsletter. (Note: Multilingual Matters books are expensive academic publications so it may be best to seek them out in a library).

National Centre for Language and Literacy (NCLL)

University of Reading
Bulmershe Court
Reading RG6 1HY
Tel: 0118 378 8820
Fax: 0118 378 6801
ncll@reading.ac.uk
www.ncll.org.uk

The National Centre for Language and Literacy serves a national audience and is concerned with all aspects of language and literacy learning. It supports teachers, parents and governors in a wide range of ways – through its unique collection of resources, publications, including a range of resources on bilingualism and working in multilingual settings, particularly in schools, covering theory and practical applications, and an extensive programme of courses and conferences, ongoing research and a membership scheme designed to meet the needs of individual schools.

The National Centre for Research in Children's Literature (NCRCL)

Froebel College
Roehampton University
Roehampton Lane
London SW15 5PJ
Tel: 020 8392 3014
www.ncrcl.ac.uk

NCRCL facilitates and supports research exchange in the field of children's literature. Based at Roehampton University, it houses several reference collections that are held in the Children's Literature Collections and in the Froebel Archive for Childhood Studies. The collections consist of bibliographical and critical works, books of historical interest from the 19th to early 20th century, and a selection of current children's books, usually prizewinners, that are added to the collection each year. Whilst the main emphasis is on British children's books, there are also materials from other countries, in particular a strong collection of contemporary Japanese picture books, as well as a growing collection of European and world children's books in translation into English.

Poetry Translation Centre

London University
Room 404, School for Oriental and African Studies
Thornhaugh Street
London WC1H 0XG
Tel: 020 7898 4367
Fax: 020 7898 4239
ptc@soas.ac.uk
www.poetrytranslation.soas.ac.uk

The Poetry Translation Centre was set up to enrich poetry in English through making good translations of non-European poetry widely available and to give readers a deeper insight into the cultural history and background informing non-European poetry in a wide variety of languages.

Seven Stories, the Centre for Children's Books

30 Lime Street
Ouseburn Valley
Newcastle-upon-Tyne
NE1 2PQ
Tel: 0845 271 0777
Fax: 0191 261 1931
www.sevenstories.org.uk

The Seven Stories Centre, housed in a converted Victorian mill in the Ouseburn Valley, Newcastle-upon-Tyne, will celebrate the children's book and its creation by establishing a unique cultural centre that will place children, young people and their books at the heart of our national culture. A national collection of manuscripts and original artwork of Britain's highly acclaimed modern children's authors and illustrators will be created. The Centre will host an exciting programme of exhibitions and arts events and make this unique resource accessible to the widest possible audiences by actively engaging with the community.

The Translators Association

The Society of Authors
84 Drayton Gardens
London SW10 9SB
Tel: 020 7373 6642
info@societyofauthors.org
www.societyofauthors.org/translators/index.htm

The Translators Association was set up in 1958 as a constituent part of the Society of Authors, a trade union for professional writers. The Translation Association is a source of professional advice.

Organisations International

Biennial of Illustration Bratislava

BIBIANA, The International House of Art for Children
BIB Secretariate
Panská ul. 41
815 39 Bratislava
Slovak Republic
www.bibiana.sk

BIB was set up in 1967 and is an important international competition that reviews original children's book illustrations. Its aim is to present the best works from different countries in the area of illustration for children and to give illustrators a chance to present their work and show it to experts and publishers. Every country can enter a maximum of 20 artists. The international jury awards prizes – Grand Prix BIB, 5 Golden Apples, 5 Plaques and contingent Honourable Mention for publishing houses.

Books and Reading for Intercultural Education (BARFIE)

House of Children's Literature
Kinderliteraturhaus, AT
Mayerhofgasse 6, A-1040
Wien, Austria
www.barfie.net

Books and Reading for Intercultural Education is a European Comenius Network of institutions from Austria, Belgium, Bulgaria, the Czech Republic, Finland, France, Poland, Portugal, Slovakia, Spain and the UK, working with children's books and media. The website has information about all the different projects, a searchable catalogue of books, teachers' support and newsletters.

Bologna Children's Book Fair, Italy

Fiera del Libro per Ragazzi
Piazza Costituzione 6
40128 Bologna, Italy
dir.com@bolognafiere.it
www.bolognafiere.it

The Bologna Children's Book Fair is held annually in April of each year. It is the leading children's publishing event amongst the world's producers of children's books, TV and film and licensing developers. It is a forum that thoroughly addresses every aspect of this field.

European Picture Book Collection (EPBC)

www.ncrcl.ac.uk

The idea of The European Picture Book Collection was conceived by Dr Penni Cotton (Roehampton University) and created in1996 by European colleagues working in the field of children's literature and teacher education supported by a grant from the European Commission. The aim of the project is that the collection should comprise one picture book from each country, decided upon after a specific selection process.

International Board on Books for Young People (IBBY)

Nonnenweg 12, Postfach
CH – 4003 Basel, Switzerland
Tel: + 4161 272 27 17
Fax: + 4161 272 27 57
ibby@ibby.org
www.ibby.org

IBBY was founded in 1953 in Zurich, Switzerland as an international network which acts as a forum for people working in all areas connected with children's books and reading. It is responsible for the Hans Christian Andersen Awards, maintains the IBBY documentation centre for disabled young people, compiles biennial IBBY honour list of outstanding children's books published in member countries, publishes *Bookbird*, organises a biennial International Congress, and is committed to supporting the growth of children's literature and literacy in developing countries.

The International Youth Library

Schloss Blutenburg D–81247
Munich, Germany
Tel: + 49 89 8912110
Fax: + 49 89 8117553
bib@ijb.de www.ijb.de

The International Youth Library, established in 1949 by Jella Lepman, is the largest library for international children's and youth literature in the world. It publishes an annual annotated catalogue, *White Ravens*, of about 250 new international children's books as well as producing other booklists, and a variety of travelling exhibitions.

NLPVF – Foundation for the Production and Translation of Dutch Literature

Singel 464
NL–1017 AW Amsterdam
Tel: +31 20 620 62 61
Fax: +31 20 620 71 79
Office@nlpvf.nl

www.nlpvf.nl/basic/NLPVF

The Foundation for the Production and Translation of Dutch Literature exists to promote interest in Dutch-language literature abroad. Foreign publishers wishing to publish translations of Dutch or Frisian literature, including children's literature and quality non-fiction, may apply for a subsidy towards the translation costs.

UNESCO Clearing House for Literary Translation

www.unesco.org (Literature and Translation, culture)

UNESCO Clearing House for Literary Translation is an initiative developed in the framework of the Global Alliance for Cultural Diversity, a centre for information, guidance and encounter for all those (translators, publishers, researchers, archivists, teachers) who work on the discovery and promotion of still unknown literatures.

Youth Festival – L'Institut français

Cultural Centre
17 Queensberry Place
London SW7 2DT
Tel: 020 7073 1350
Fax: 020 7073 1355
www.institut-francais.org.uk

An annual Youth Festival organised by l'Institut français takes place in November with French and British authors and illustrators. The Festival runs for three days. The first two are school days with a range of activities including general sessions in Ciné Lumière, workshops, screenings, discussions and an exhibition. The last day is a 'Fun Day' open to the general public.

Websites

The Danish Literature Centre

The Danish Arts Agency
Kongens Nytorv 3
DK-1050 Copenhagen K
literature@danish-arts.dk
www.literaturenet.dk

The Danish Literature Centre was set up in 1997 and set up the literaturenet website to make Danish literature in translation accessible to a wider public. It contains profiles on Danish authors, a section on the history of Danish and an edited link guide to Danish literature on the Net.

East European countries visit www.literarytranslation. com/resources/links

French Book News

www.frenchbooknews.org.uk

French Book News provides English language publishers with information on new publications in French and translations in French.

German literature online

www.litrix.de

Litrix.de is a project initiated by the Federal Cultural Foundation and supported by the Goethe-Institut with the aim of promoting an appreciation of contemporary German literature and its translation. It contains extensive specimen texts and translations as well as portraits of writers and their works.

www.literarytranslation. com/art

A joint project by the British Council and British Centre for Literary Translation, it aims to celebrate the art of translation and bring to a new audience an appreciation of the complexities and richness of this art form.

AFTERWORD
Deborah Hallford

'It is a sign of the parochialism of the British literary scene that foreign literature is so neglected . . . To an outsider the British publishing industry can seem like a conspiracy intent on depriving English-speaking readers of the majority of good books written in other languages than their own'

'Lost in Translation', extract of speech by John Carey, Bookseller.com 30/06/05

In the light of Professor John Carey's observations in his speech on 27th June at the *Man Booker International Prize* 2005, it is important to look at why Britain has become so culturally insular and how this trend can be reversed. *Outside In* has explored the reasons why literature in translation is so important, and why we must work towards encouraging more publishers to translate foreign literature.

While there are some positive signs, with more small publishers taking the lead, new ventures like WingedChariot Press – which is an exciting development in the UK publishing industry – and a few dedicated children's publishers continuing to add to their list of translated titles or reissuing classics, other publishers are conspicuous by their absence.

For those publishers that do undertake translation it is disappointing that they sometimes feel the need to 'anglicise' stories, names of places and characters for an UK audience. This somehow seems to suggest that UK children are unable to deal with the 'foreignness' contained in a book. Anglicisation of authors' names is even worse! This merely panders to the widespread belief of the stereotypical viewpoint that Aidan Chambers so eloquently articulated in his speech at the 2005 *Marsh Award for Children's Literature in Translation*. 'Publishers don't publish more translations, and especially not those books very different from our own, because they don't sell. They don't sell because there is an ingrained Anglo-American prejudice against translation'. ('An Indispensable Heritage', School Librarian, Spring 2005.)

There must be many books for children and adults in other languages that could easily become commercial successes if publishers were prepared to take the plunge. With marketing budgets reserved for the big-name authors in the UK it is difficult to see how this trend might change. Even if publishers have a translated author on their list, the book may disappear into oblivion if it is not actively promoted.

There are, of course, grants available to publishers for translation projects and these can go someway to assisting with the additional costs of production. However, there needs to be a much greater awareness of the variety of books that are out there waiting to be translated and which could be turned into a viable success. It is important for booksellers to be much more aware of the translated titles that are currently available in the UK and actively promote them. Events such as the Children's Bookshow, the work of IBBY, the Centre for British Translation, the *Marsh Award for Children's Literature in Translation* and many other organisations working on projects in this area, go some way towards highlighting the importance of translated children's literature. However, much more still needs to be done.

Now we come to the oft forgotten role of the translator. With a few exceptions the translator is generally invisible. This has been highlighted in the compilation of this publication by the limited translator biographies at the back of the guide. Sadly, we were unable to be as comprehensive as we would have liked due to the lack of information available from publishers. Some books do not acknowledge a translator at all; others are mentioned in the minute print in the bibliographical information. More enlightened publishers credit the translator on the title page along with the author, however, only a handful provide biographical details of the translator. This is really something that publishers must address. All books should carry details about the author, illustrator and translator, however brief. One of the really surprising things to find was that some books had no details about the author either! If we want children and young people to read translated authors from other countries, why do we assume that they won't want to know about the author who wrote the book?

The translator has to come up with an accurate version of the original work in a way that also captures the spirit. They are as important as the author and as Lene Kaaberbol has said 'At its best a translation is an independent creation that breathes and vibrates in its second language incarnation. What it is not is a perfect copy'. ('Only this time, in English', Carousel, Summer 2003)

Rosemary Goring rather bluntly suggested in an article for The Glasgow Herald, that a translator, 'in the world of literature, and of fiction in particular . . . is little more conspicuous than a roadsweeper, and not much better paid', She goes on to revise this view, comparing them to miners 'picking away, out of sight, at seams of gold' and suggests that they should be rightly acknowledged and 'met with a fanfare of trumpets and a wave of applause from' . . . 'It is the very least they deserve'. (Forget the cheesemakers, blessed are the Translators', 24/01/05)

With the exception of the dual-language titles there are only a handful of books outside Europe – Argentina, Brazil, French Canadian Quebec, India, Iraq, Israel, Japan and Turkey – that appear in this guide. This is because there are hardly any books translated from countries outside Europe. Even within Europe, the omissions are noticeable – only one book from both Greece and Italy, two picture books from Portugal, one poetry book from former Eastern Europe and nothing from Spain or the Baltic states. This is disappointing and there should be many, many more countries represented here. With an enlarged Europe now, we need to see more translations from all of these countries as well as the rest of the world.

There are a great many wonderful books out there waiting to be brought to an UK audience. We hope that this guide will go some way to encourage publishers to identify gaps in this area and to translate more children's literature.

'For every reader some such shock of foreignness is salutary. For the nation, especially if that nation is English-speaking, the continued shock of the foreign is absolutely indispensable'

David Constantine, A Living Language, 'Translation is Good for You', Bloodaxe, 2004

Index Titles

	Title	Country	Page No:

Index Titles